"Flannigan, you j̲____ ___ ___ __ anymore," Tess said, tipping the champagne glass toward her lips.

"If I wanted to, I could make you eat those words." Mick reached and caught her wrist as the first golden drop fell onto her tongue. Lord, she was tempting.

"Fortunately for you, I'm not in the mood," he said, letting her go.

"Well, now . . ." She settled back into her chair and circled her tongue around her lips. When they were glistening with champagne, she smiled. "We've established that we're not attracted to each other anymore. What else is there to talk about?"

"We used to have plenty to talk about. . . ." Mick's voice trailed off as he gazed at Tess's skin and noted how her pulse fluttered at the base of her throat, like spring leaves dancing in a breeze. She wore a creamy satin gown and outrageously sequined shoes that sparkled when she moved.

His throat grew tight. "Remember the time I drank from your shoe?"

The sudden sound of his voice startled her, forced her to look up. Mick's face had that intense, brooding look he had always got just before they made love. Slowly he reached down and caught her ankle. His thumb drew circles on her leg as he lifted it to his lap.

Tess felt as if all her nerve endings were centered in the spot he touched. She had lied to him. From the minute he'd walked into the kitchen she'd wanted to rake her fingernails down his chest and feel the tight muscles underneath his gleaming skin. Just long enough to see if it felt as good as she remembered. . . .

WHAT ARE *LOVESWEPT* ROMANCES?

They are stories of true romance and touching emotion. We believe those two very important ingredients are constants in our highly sensual and very believable stories in the *LOVESWEPT* line. Our goal is to give you, the reader, stories of consistently high quality that may sometimes make you laugh, sometimes make you cry, but are always fresh and creative and contain many delightful surprises within their pages.

Most romance fans read an enormous number of books. Those they truly love, they keep. Others may be traded with friends and soon forgotten. We hope that each *LOVESWEPT* romance will be a treasure—a "keeper." We will always try to publish

LOVE STORIES YOU'LL NEVER FORGET
BY AUTHORS YOU'LL ALWAYS REMEMBER

The Editors

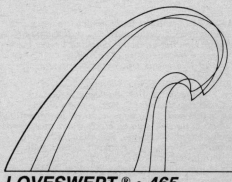

LOVESWEPT ® • 465

Peggy Webb
That Jones Girl

![Bantam rooster logo] **BANTAM BOOKS**
NEW YORK · TORONTO · LONDON · SYDNEY · AUCKLAND

THAT JONES GIRL
A Bantam Book / April 1991

If you would be interested in receiving protective vinyl
covers for your Loveswept books, please write to this
address for information:

Loveswept
Bantam Books
P.O. Box 985
Hicksville, NY 11802

ISBN 0-553-44108-6

Published simultaneously in the United States and Canada

PRINTED IN THE UNITED STATES OF AMERICA

OPM 0 9 8 7 6 5 4 3 2 1

Prologue

Tess Jones Flannigan Carson O'Toole was sound asleep. Sprawled across her bed, she slept as if she were on an island splashed with vivid color and surrounded by an ocean of raucous sound. Her hair was a spill of red on the pillow, her silk gown a ripple of purple. One high-heeled slipper, hanging precariously from her toe, sparkled with gold sequins. The hands on her clock radio pointed to 2:00 P.M., and a rock and roll song blared.

Tess slept on.

A Siamese cat sat on the windowsill, switching his tail and watching his mistress. After a long perusal, he leaped from his perch to a nearby chair and from there made a flying leap to the pillow. He sat like a silent Buddha for a while, then leaned down and licked his mistress's bare shoulder.

She stirred. The cat's pink tongue glided over her skin again.

"O'Toole. Is that you?"

Tess rolled over slowly, yawning and stretching. Giving a cat-smile of satisfaction, O'Toole made himself more comfortable on the pillow and began to wash his paws.

"I guess I'd oversleep every day if it weren't for you." She leaned over and rubbed his head. "Thanks, O'Toole."

O'Toole continued his bath as if he didn't care whether she thanked him or not. Tess laughed. Her cat was just like her last husband: A bulldozer could have rolled over the bed, and neither of them would have shown a speck of emotion. After she'd packed Robert O'Toole's bags and sent him on his way, she'd acquired the Siamese, named him O'Toole to remind herself that she'd already made three mistakes and she'd better be careful with husband number four—whoever he might be.

Tess battled her way out of her fluffy bed—everything was duck down and soft and deep and cuddly, just the way she liked it. She walked around her bedroom lopsided, searching for her other shoe. It was hanging from the hat rack, its sequins sparkling in the bright sunlight that poured through the window.

Tess took it off without blinking an eye, as if shoes were supposed to be on a hat rack. Humming a New Orleans blues song, she put on her shoe, tossed her peignoir carelessly over her shoulders, and went into her den, trailing purple chiffon and ostrich plumes.

Her intercom buzzed.

"Telegram for Miss Jones."

She smiled. It was probably from one of her fans. She was always getting mail and flowers from her fans.

"Come on up."

The delivery boy from Western Union handed the telegram to Tess and stayed to watch her read. She was his favorite singer and probably his favorite person in all of Chicago. Miss Tess Jones had style.

A tiny frown creased her forehead as she read.

"Bad news, Miss Jones?"

"I'm afraid so." She folded the telegram into a neat square, her long fingernails bright red against the stark white paper. "A good friend of mine back home has died."

"Gee, that's too bad." He took off his cap in deference to the dead. "I'm sorry, Miss Jones."

"Thanks, Henry."

"I guess you'll be going home for the funeral?"

Tess Jones Flannigan Carson O'Toole did an extraordinary thing, astonishing Henry so he almost dropped his cap: She smiled.

"I'll be going home, all right, Henry. But not for a funeral. I'll be going home for a celebration."

Then she explained to him.

"There were six of us, three boys and three girls, best of friends, the rowdiest group on the college campus. If a water balloon fell on a professor, everybody knew that one of us had done it. If a rival college's mascot was stolen, the group was automatically given credit." She paused, smiling at the good memories.

"We lived high and fast and hard and well. And we made a pact that when one of us died, the survivors would gather and have a great going-away party."

"A going-away party, Miss Jones?"

Tess reached out and patted his cheek. "Death is merely a journey from one realm to another. Remember that, Henry."

After Henry had gone, Tess leaned against the door, tapping the telegram with her fingernails. Suddenly she shivered. But not for death, not for Babs. Babs had died the way she had lived—with style. According to Johnny's telegram, she'd crashed her plane into the Rockies. Death had come instantly, quick and clean and neat.

No. She shivered not for Babs but for herself. All the members of the group would come. There was no doubt about it. Flannigan would be there. If Johnny could find him, Mick Flannigan would be in Tupelo, Mississippi.

She leaned against the door, remembering. Mick Flannigan, her best friend forever, her first lover, her first love. The man who had walked out on her ten years ago after only six months of marriage.

"Damn you, Mick Flannigan." Tess wadded the telegram into a ball and tossed it across the room. "I didn't cry for you then, and I won't cry for you now."

Trailing purple chiffon and ostrich feathers and the heavenly scent of jasmine, she went to her telephone to make arrangements.

One

Mick Flannigan was not prepared for his first sight of Tess.

He lounged against a Greek column on Johnny and Babs's front porch and watched Tess get out of the taxi and come up the brick pathway. She had been beautiful ten years ago, but now she was astonishing. Her red hair was longer and fuller. The setting summer sun caught sparks in it, giving her a halo of flame. Her eyes were the same—green, long-lashed, and mysteriously slanted. Her walk was the same too. She still walked as if she owned the world.

It was her face that caught his attention. Time had sculpted the cheekbones, refined the features. At twenty-five Tess had had the soft, dewy look of a rose in first bloom. Now, she was one of the exotics, a passion flower, sleek and perfect and rare.

Regret sliced through him, and then he reminded himself that it was too late for regret. Ten years too late.

He took his cigar from his mouth and exhaled deeply, watching her through the smoke rings.

With one slim foot poised on the top step, Tess stopped. She turned her head slowly, like a wild creature sensing a trap.

Flannigan stepped out of the shadows.

"Hello, Tess."

Her nostrils flared briefly, then she offered her hand, a princess doling out favors to one of her lowly subjects.

"Flannigan."

That was all she said. "Flannigan." She used to call him Mick unless she was mad at him—or unless they were making love. In the throes of passion she would say his name over and over. "Flannigan . . . Flannigan . . . Flannigan . . ." He wondered what was going through her mind now.

He took her hand in his and held it for a long moment, gazing deeply into her eyes. They told him nothing. He didn't know what he had expected, but certainly something more than this cool greeting that she might have given a complete stranger.

Turning her hand over, he leaned down and pressed a kiss in her palm. For the sheer wickedness of it, he circled his tongue over her warm skin, lingering until he felt her hand tremble.

He flicked his tongue out again, and she trembled once more, but she didn't pull away. The lady had guts. He had always admired that about her.

"Ten years hasn't changed you at all, has it, Flannigan? You're still using your charm on everything in skirts."

"Are you charmed, Tess?" He straightened up and smiled at her.

It was the smile she remembered so well. She

used to think that surely the angels bent down and sighed when Mick Flannigan smiled. Now, she thought it was practiced, too smooth, too perfect, too calculated.

"Not anymore, Flannigan. I got over being charmed by you when you picked up your bags and walked out on me." His smile vanished, and now it was her turn. She gave him her most brilliant, most enchanting stage smile, the one she used to win over cold audiences. "But what the heck—bygones are bygones. There's no need for us to let our little mistake spoil this weekend." She reached over and pinched his cheek. "Will you be a sweetheart, Flannigan, and bring in my bags?" She started into the house, then turned and said over her shoulder, "Be careful with the cage. I don't want to upset O'Toole."

"Who the hell is O'Toole?"

"He was my third husband, but now he's my cat."

She swept into the house without a backward glance.

Flannigan felt as if he'd just survived a hurricane. Her third husband. Damn. She changed husbands as often as she did nightgowns. And she'd named her cat after that fool O'Toole, whoever he was. He wondered if she'd named anything Flannigan.

Not that it mattered. He clamped his cigar between his teeth and strode down the walk. Her belongings were piled high—four bags in all, including the cat cage—waiting for some besotted fool to carry them in. Not that he was besotted by her, not by a long shot. But it amused him to see that Tess was still giving commands. She had always had a following of people, mostly men, waiting to do her bidding.

He propped a booted foot on one of her bags and took a long, thoughtful drag on his cigar. She had called their marriage "a little mistake." Funny how that hurt. All these years he'd thought that first love was the sweetest and the best, and she'd thought it was "a little mistake."

"What difference does it make now? The past is over and done with." He blew three smoke rings in the air, then clamped his cigar between his teeth and picked up her bags.

The group would be waiting for him.

Johnny Kalinopolis sat in his den, surrounded by his friends who had come from all over the world to help him send his beloved Babs off in style.

Tess had purposely stationed herself on the sofa next to Johnny so her back would be to the front door. She didn't want to see Flannigan when he came into the house. Damn, he looked good. He had always been devastatingly handsome. That hadn't changed. He still had eyes so blue they looked like a bit of the sky, and his black hair was still wild and tousled, curling just enough to make a woman itch to get her hands in it.

But it wasn't his looks that had her running a bit scared. It was something else, something she couldn't define. Some gut instinct told Tess that this older Flannigan should be wearing a warning sign—a neon billboard reading DANGER. DO NOT TOUCH.

She turned her attention back to the group. Lovey and Jim Hawkins had been the first to marry. With the rest of the group standing by, they had said vows their sophomore year of college. And now Lovey was in an easy chair with Jim sitting on the ottoman at her feet, holding her hand. Tess envied them.

"You two look as much in love as you did the day you got married," Tess said. "Remember that day, Lovey?"

"How could I forget?" Lovey laughed. "Jim was terrified."

"But not of marriage, my pet." Jim patted her stomach, big with their fourth child. "I was afraid you were going to deliver the baby right there in the JP's office before we could say the vows."

"Didn't you have any confidence in your friends?" Johnny leaned over and punched Jim's shoulder. "I was all set to deliver, and Mick was standing by in case I needed any help."

"He was standing by in a hearse." Lovey hooted with laughter. "Do you remember the look on the doctor's face when I climbed down from that crazy old vehicle, trailing rose petals and a white veil. I wonder whatever happened to the hearse?"

"It went to its final resting place at the bottom of the Tombigbee River." Mick's booming voice preceded him into the room. His boots, tromping across the hardwood floor, punctuated his words. "Both of us were loaded with scotch at the time."

He piled the bags at the foot of the stairs, put out his cigar, then strode toward the sofa. When he was standing only a few inches from Tess, he paused, smiling down at her.

"I believe I have something you want, Tess, my girl."

"Flannigan, I wouldn't want anything you had if it were delivered to me on a silver platter."

The room became hushed with expectation as Johnny, Lovey, and Jim watched their two old friends square off. Their tempers were legend. In the halcyon days of their youth their stormy courtship had often been a source of amusement and wonder to the rest of the group.

They watched as Mick suddenly leaned so close to Tess, his lips were almost against her cheek.

"Nobody's ever tried to put it on a silver platter. I guess they couldn't find one big enough."

"I see that age has not diminished your ego."

"Or my charm." Mick straightened up, laughing. Then he produced the cat cage from behind his back. "This is what I was referring to, my love. Your cat."

"I knew that all along." She reached for the cage, but Mick held it beyond her grasp.

"I never do a favor without exacting a price."

"Name it." Tess stood up and faced him, nose to nose. Women used to fall like tenpins for Mick Flannigan, especially the timid, shy women, Tess mused. The only way to survive around him was to be strong. She had survived Mick Flannigan once: This time she planned to triumph. "No price you can name is beyond my pocketbook—or my power."

"Then this should be easy for you." Keeping the cat cage in his hand, Mick made himself comfortable in an easy chair. "Sing for me."

"That's a great idea," said Johnny, rising from the sofa. "Wait a minute. Let me get Babs." He disappeared from the room and came back carrying an urn. Holding his wife's ashes, he sat back down on the sofa. "Now, the group is complete. Carry on."

"Jim, will you play?" Tess walked across the room and leaned against the baby grand piano, facing Mick. "What would you have me sing?"

"'It Had to be You'." Mick's expression never changed as he named the song Tess had been singing when they had first met.

She had been singing in a small club off campus to earn her way through college. Mick Flannigan had walked through the door, his blue eyes never leaving hers as he made his way to the table beside the stage. From that moment on she sang just for him.

Now, looking into his eyes, she knew that all the songs of her life had been sung for Mick Flannigan. Even after he'd left her, the haunting memory of him in that smoky, crowded nightclub had stayed with her.

Damn you, Mick Flannigan, she thought. *I won't fall under your spell again.*

"Key of C, Jim."

Tess's eyes never left Mick's as the first blues notes rose from the keyboard and drifted around her. The music entered her body, her heart, her soul. A languor stole over her, and she began to sing. With her hips pressed intimately against the piano, she lifted her mass of hair off her neck with one arm. All her movements were natural and uncalculated. She was lost in song, totally unaware of her impact on her audience.

Mick felt as if his heart were trapped under a boulder. He reached for his cigar, hoping his hands didn't shake. *Dear Lord,* he thought as he struck a match on the heel of his boot. *She still makes love to her audience when she sings.*

He watched her through a cloud of blue smoke, but the smoke screen didn't diminish her impact. He cursed himself for asking her to sing. Hell, he was too old and too wise to be playing with fire, especially the Tess Jones brand of fire. That Jones girl had always been too hot to handle. And that Jones woman . . . His mind boggled trying to think what it would be like to handle her.

Whoa, Flannigan. Back off.

He settled back into his chair and tried to feign polite interest. He hoped he was fooling his friends. They had told him, one by one, that divorcing Tess was a mistake. He had to prove them wrong.

"Mick. Mick?"

Suddenly he realized that Tess had finished singing and Johnny was talking to him.

"I'm sorry, Johnny. What did you say?"

"I asked if you still played the harmonica."

"Yes. In fact, it's the same old blues harp I used to tote around in my pocket back in our days at Mississippi State."

"Do something together for us, you and Tess, like you used to do."

Mick was on the verge of refusing, then Johnny added, "Babs loved hearing the two of you. She used to say listening to you and Tess make music was like dying and going to heaven."

"Tess?" said Mick, glancing across the room for confirmation.

"I'm game if you are, Flannigan." He stood up, then Tess added, "But you have to do something for me first."

"I'm your slave. Name it."

"Let O'Toole out of the cage."

"Your third husband or the cat?" Flannigan quipped as he unlatched the cage door.

"Sometimes I think they are one and the same. Both of them are beasts."

The rest of the group laughed and Flannigan smiled, but he didn't think it was all that funny. As a matter of fact, the more he thought about it, the more he hated the idea of Tess's third husband being a beast. Did that mean he had been a tiger in bed? He suddenly discovered that he didn't like the idea of Tess in anybody's bed, let alone a beast's. Three husbands. Dammit.

He had never married again. Over the years he'd pictured Tess unmarried, too, working hard at her career, perhaps pining a little for him. He wished he'd never found out about her other husbands.

He stalked across the room, not stopping until he was so close to Tess he could see that wicked amber starburst in the center of her green eyes and smell the jasmine on her skin.

"You remember how we did this, don't you, Tess, my girl?"

"Yes. You played. I sang."

"Ahh, my pretty one. Your memory grows weak with age."

Flannigan hooked the piano bench with his boot and dragged it across the floor. In one smooth motion he sat down, drawing her into his lap.

"You always sat in my lap. Remember?"

"I remember." Grinning wickedly, Tess leaned so close, the tip of her nose touched his. "But Flannigan . . . I fear your lap has grown weak with age."

The rest of the group roared with laughter. The very devil danced in Flannigan's blue eyes as he tipped Tess's chin up with one finger.

"Careful, Tess, my darlin'. I might have to prove you wrong."

"In that case, Flannigan—she paused, reaching up to run her fingers through his hair—you're the one who should be careful."

Two

"I was never cautious, Tess." He locked his hands around her wrists. For a moment his eyes held hers; then he added, too softly for the rest of the group to hear, ". . . especially with you."

"What do you mean to do, Flannigan? Put me in handcuffs?"

"It's a thought."

Tess had always had a way of gearing up for battle: Her nostrils flared slightly, her eyes turned a brighter shade of green, and her muscles tensed. He could see the signs now, and while he was not cautious, he was sometimes prudent. This was not the time for a battle, especially a battle with Tess Jones.

He reached into his pocket to pull out his harmonica, and Tess gave him an arch smile. They were at a standoff now, with her having the edge. Both of them knew it.

He .played a few experimental chords on the blues harp, then smiled at her.

"Are you ready, Tess?"

"I'm always ready. You're the one who needs warming up."

Without consulting her on the tune, he played the opening bars of "Stormy Weather." She leaned back with a satisfied smile on her face, and when it was time, she began to sing.

He was going to have to be careful all right. He was still hearing siren songs, and right now hers was the most enchanting of all. Ahhh, but it wouldn't last. He was restless, restless, always on the move. And he was no more willing to drag her around while he searched for his elusive rainbow than he had been ten years ago.

Tess drew him like a magnet, played him like a piano. It had always been that way with them. She would walk into a room, and he automatically gravitated toward her. Even after they had first met, when neither of them wanted to fall in love, they hadn't been able to stay away from each other. If he wanted to hop into his hearse and drive to the pool hall for a lively game, he called Tess. And if she wanted to stay up all night eating popcorn and watching horror movies on TV, she called him. That's the way they had been—best friends who hadn't fallen in love as much as come to a realization that they had always been in love.

He continued playing. *Get this over and done with*, he told himself. *Then get out of Tupelo and don't look back*. He had survived all those years without Tess by never looking back.

He and Tess did three songs, each one harder to endure than the one before. He wished he'd never pulled her onto his lap. But it was too late now. Fortunately Lovey and Jim and Johnny didn't seem to notice that anything was going on except the music.

And when it was all over, Tess rose from his lap

like some damned queen, then turned around and shook his hand. Shook his hand! Ah, she was a cool one all right.

"If you ever need a job as my backup, call me, Mick."

"If I ever call you again, it won't be for a job."

"Then you should be prepared to stand in line."

"You have lots of gentlemen callers, do you?"

"Yes, but most of them aren't gentlemen. I prefer the wild type."

"You always did."

He pulled a cigar out of his pocket, then leaned down and struck a match on his boot. Cupping the light with his hands, he lit his cigar and took a long, thoughtful draw. Seeing her through the blue smoke didn't make her any less vivid. If anything, it made her more real to him. During their college days he was always seeing her through the blue haze of smoke in some small nightclub, watching from afar as she dazzled her audience from a tiny stage.

"I guess I was the wildest of all," he added, needing to know.

"Well"—she cocked her head to one side and considered for a long time, long enough to make him wish he hadn't added that last comment—"actually, Flannigan, I think the honor goes to my second husband. Carson made the hounds of hell seem tame." With that parting shot, she left.

He clamped his teeth hard on his cigar and almost bit the end off. *Carson.* What in the hell kind of name was that? It sounded sissy to him. Anyway, he hadn't wanted to know the name of her second husband. Next thing you knew, she'd be naming her lovers.

She had walked across the room and was standing by Lovey now. He sighed in relief and took a long draw on his cigar, studying her through the smoke rings. He wondered if she'd had lovers too. A woman like Tess—

"I'll bet everybody's starving," said Johnny, interrupting Flannigan's train of thought. "There's enough food in the kitchen to feed everybody in Tupelo. You know how it is when somebody . . . passes on."

His refusal to mention death was not like Johnny. His friends noticed. Of all the group, he was the most pragmatic, the most forthright. Besides, he was a doctor. Death was something he saw every day. By using a euphemism, he'd told them exactly how much Babs's death had affected him.

He led them into the kitchen, still talking.

"Most people can't quite bring themselves to come right out and say what they're feeling, so they make piles of food to let the bereaved know they care. A lovely custom."

They scattered around the kitchen, getting paper plates and filling glasses with ice and trying to identify casseroles—all with good-natured jostling and joking.

"This one looks suspiciously like corn." Jim held up a dish for his wife to see. "Do you think that's corn, Lovey?"

"It could be, sweetheart." She leaned over and took a long whiff. "Mmm, smells divine. You should try it."

"You know I can't abide corn."

Laughing, Lovey set the casserole on the table among all the other casseroles and pies and cakes and sandwiches and pickles.

"It's a feast," Flannigan said.

"Wouldn't she have loved it?" Johnny asked, smiling at each of his friends around the table. "Wait a minute. Where's Babs?"

"I thought you were bringing her," Tess said.

"Well, I set her on the piano for a minute . . . Hold everything. Don't say a thing important. I'll be right back."

Johnny came back and put the urn in a place of honor at the head of the table. The group grew quiet. Jim slipped his arm around Lovey's waist, and Johnny hovered close to his wife's ashes.

Tess glanced across the room at Mick. He was leaning against the wall, his face gone dark and sober. Suddenly she felt very much alone. She pictured herself, spinning out her years, trailing them thinly behind her like so many bits of colored yarn. And when she was gone, somebody would pick up her purple peignoir and her gold shoes and say, "Is this all that's left of Tess? Had she no children? No husband? No one who's going to miss her? Is this all there is of Tess Jones Flannigan Carson O'Toole?"

She didn't like to picture herself vanishing, dying and being practically invisible. Maybe it shouldn't be that way. Maybe her cat would live as long as she did. Maybe he would sit in front of her urn, licking his paws and pretending he didn't care, but all the same missing her terribly and nursing a broken heart.

She glanced at Flannigan again. He seemed bigger, more vital, more powerful, more *real* than when she last looked his way. Funny how death magnified the living.

"I'm mad at her, you know," Johnny said quietly. "She wasn't supposed to leave me to face the years alone."

"Anger is natural, Johnny. You'll probably even feel some guilt. Most survivors do." Jim was the one talking.

During their college days he had always been the

one to explain their feelings and rationalize their moods. He was a clinical psychologist now with a booming practice. And no wonder, Tess thought. She felt better already. She'd been a little angry at Babs herself.

"What do you think she's doing now?" Johnny asked.

The group was very quiet, watching him. Jim and Lovey sat side by side on straight-backed chairs, holding on to each other as if death threatened them. Tess felt a chill creeping into the room. She wanted to push it back, kicking and screaming that it had no business there in Tupelo at the going-away party. But all she could do was look at the urn.

"Hell, Kalinopolis." Flannigan's voice boomed around the room, dispelling the gloom. He pushed himself away from the wall and strode across the kitchen. When he reached Tess, he casually draped his arm over her shoulder. "She's out there somewhere talking about flying with Amelia Earhart and Charles Lindbergh."

Tess took her cue. She and Flannigan had always worked as a team, keeping a banter going when the group needed perking up.

"If they gave her wings," she chimed in, "she's already striped them blue and gold and painted *The Johnny K.* in big black letters across their sides. You know she never had a flying machine she didn't name *The Johnny K.*"

Johnny and Jim and Lovey began to smile. Flannigan and Tess continued their banter.

"Remember that time she bombed the Sigma Chi house?" said Flannigan, squeezing Tess's arm. She knew the signal. It was her turn.

"It took us a month to find all those plastic donkeys."

"You were in on that?"

"Heck, yes. Did you think Babs would have had the patience to go round up one hundred plastic donkeys and cut their backsides off?"

The group hooted with laughter.

"You should have seen their faces the next day when they told about it," Johnny said. "The back-ends of all those plastic donkeys falling out of the sky, and Babs buzzing so low, they thought she was going to take the roof off their frat house."

"Served them right," Lovey said. "The very idea. Not inviting the smartest man on campus to join their fraternity."

"I can hardly blame them. All I needed was a mustache and a gun to look like I'd just left the Family back in Greece."

They began to talk at once, bringing Babs gently back into their midst by telling old stories of their youthful escapades.

Out of the corner of his eyes, Flannigan could see Tess's red hair. The subtle fragrance of flowers filled his senses. Being close to her felt too good. He took his arm from around her shoulders and eased away. But not too far.

She was a part of the group, an old friend. Surely he could sit close to an old friend for a few hours while they reminisced. He kept telling himself that. Over and over.

When he discovered he was leaning closer just to hear the whispery, bluesy sound of her voice better, he reminded himself that it was friendship he was feeling—and nostalgia. When his hand touched hers as he passed the chocolate cake, he told himself it was only natural her hands should feel different, softer, sweeter, more *electric* than any other woman's hand. After all, they had once been husband and wife. They were the last to leave the kitchen.

Tess licked one last bit of chocolate icing from her fingers and smiled at Flannigan.

"You were wonderful, Mick. If you hadn't done something, all of us would have been crying in another minute."

"You weren't so bad yourself, Tess, my girl."

He leaned down and kissed her on the cheek.

"You taste like chocolate."

"Chocolate used to be your favorite flavor."

"It still is." He tipped her face up with the back of his hand. In the fluorescent glare of the kitchen light they studied each other for a long time. His face was so intense, Tess thought he might be going to kiss her.

There was no question about what she would do. She'd kiss him back . . . for old time's sake.

Abruptly he released her.

"Good night, Tess, my girl."

" 'Night, Mick."

They went up the staircase together, conscious of each other and not wanting to be and not knowing what to do about it. At the top they hesitated, looking at each other. Mick started to say good night, but he'd already said that. In the end they merely nodded and went their separate ways.

Mick closed his door firmly behind him, then lay in the dark thinking about the taste of chocolate on her skin and the way her hair had swung around and touched his face when she turned her head. He didn't even try to sleep.

Across the hall, Tess tried. Lying alone on her clean sheets with her hands folded resolutely across her chest, she closed her eyes. She stayed that way for two hours, glancing at the bedside clock every now and then to see if she was making any progress.

But she couldn't fall asleep, even in the peaceful darkness of her small southern hometown, even with the tranquil murmur of crape-myrtle branches against the windowpane and the friendly patches of moonlight on the ceiling. Rather than toss and turn and, worse yet, try to name the cause of her unexpected wakefulness, she untangled herself from the covers and scooped O'Toole off the bed. He complained loudly, but she kissed the top of his head and shushed him.

"Be quiet, O'Toole, and help me find my shoes."

He was no help at all, sitting in her arms glowering, but she found them anyway and slipped them on. Then she grabbed her silk peignoir and flung it over her shoulders.

She decided to go down to the kitchen again. She'd figure out what to do once she got there. When she was growing up, her aunt Bertha had told her that most of the world's problems could be settled in a good cozy kitchen. It was one of the few things Aunt Bertha had ever said that made sense to Tess.

Her high heels sank into the plush carpet as she made her way out of the bedroom and down the stairs. The urn was sitting on the hall table next to a bouquet of gardenias. On impulse, Tess decided to take Babs with her.

"You always did love gardenias," she said as she plucked the urn off the table.

With O'Toole in one arm and Babs in the other, she had quite an armload, but Tess didn't mind. She felt better already. Having friends around always perked her up.

She put her cat and her friend on the kitchen

table and began to rummage through the cabinets.

"Do you still keep champagne here?" She searched in the back of the refrigerator—finding the bottle at last. The cork was tight and the wire over it wouldn't give. She always did have trouble with corks. That had been the only good thing about Carson, her second husband. He had been handy with corks.

"Come on," she said as she struggled with the wire. "If you cut my finger and the cork flies like a missile, I'm going to scream."

"Drinking alone, Tess?"

She almost dropped the bottle. Mick Flannigan stood in the doorway, his chest bare and his jeans as tight as sin. He was the last person she wanted to see right now. It was all his fault that she was up in the wee hours, rambling around the kitchen.

"What are you doing down here, Mick?"

"I might ask you the same thing." He took the bottle from her and deftly popped out the cork. He wasn't about to tell her that he'd been lying awake in his bed, listening for any movement from her side of the hall.

"I came down for a late-night chat with Babs."

"Will I do just as well?" He handed her the champagne, then hooked a chair with his bare foot and pulled it out for her.

"No." She sat down, then leaned back in her chair and gave him a bold once-over. "I'm not in the mood for a half-naked man tonight."

The thought of her being in the mood for any half-naked man except himself made heat climb over his chest and up his neck. He knew if he didn't rein in his temper, there would be the devil to pay. Tess could match him word for word, the hotter the better.

Hooking another chair, he sat facing her, almost close enough to touch. Almost, but not quite.

"In that case, my darling, I could shuck these jeans."

"Don't bother. I've already seen it all." She propped one elbow on the table and poured herself a glass of champagne, taking her time so that each drop seemed to come out separately and do a song-and-dance routine before it finally hit the glass. Out of the corner of her eye she could see exactly how she maddened him.

"Quite frankly, Flannigan, you don't interest me anymore." She tipped the glass toward her lips.

"If I wanted to, I could make you eat those words, my girl." He reached out and caught her wrist just as the first drop of golden liquid fell onto her tongue. Lord, she was tempting.

"Fortunately for you, I'm not in the mood," he said finally, as he let her go.

"Well, now . . ." She settled back into her chair and slowly circled her tongue around her lips. When they were glistening with champagne, she smiled at him. "We've established that we aren't attracted to each other anymore. What else is there to talk about?"

"We used to have plenty to talk about."

"That was a long time ago."

"So it was."

An uneasy silence fell upon them. To cover the awkwardness, Tess concentrated on drinking her champagne.

Mick watched her throat as she swallowed. He remembered how her skin felt under his lips, deliciously cool, even in the hottest part of summer, and how her pulse fluttered at the base of her throat, like spring leaves dancing in a breeze.

To get his mind off her skin, he leaned back in

his chair and studied her clothes. She wore a gown that would make saints lose their crowns, a bit of creamy satin dripping with ostrich plumes. Until this very moment he didn't know how much he'd missed those frothy, sexy gowns of hers. And the dancing shoes. He glanced down at her feet. She still wore those outrageous sequined shoes that sparkled when she walked.

His throat got tight, and he began to feel soft and sentimental.

"Remember the time I drank from your shoe?"

The sudden sound of his voice startled her. She set her glass carefully on the table, not looking at him. She didn't want to remember. She didn't want to be sitting in the kitchen thinking about Jim and Lovey holding hands and wondering what it would be like if she had the right to do the same thing with Flannigan.

"Remember?" he said again, so softly she was forced to look up.

His face had that intense brooding look she knew so well, the look he always got just before they made love. Slowly he reached down and caught her ankle. His thumb drew circles on her leg as he lifted it to his lap.

She felt as if all her nerve endings were centered in the spot he touched. She had lied to him. From the minute he had walked into the kitchen, she had wanted to rake her fingernails down his chest and feel the tight muscles underneath his gleaming skin. Just once. Just long enough to see if it felt as good as she remembered. Oh, it had been a whopper of a lie. She had wanted a half-naked man. She had wanted him then, and she wanted him even more now.

And where in the world did that leave her? She

might as well be in the urn with Babs than hook her star to Mick Flannigan's wagon again.

She pulled her foot out of his grasp, slowly, so he wouldn't see how he bothered her.

"You were young then," she said.

"Meaning?"

"Meaning you've grown dull in your old age."

"Dull?"

His voice sent shivers down her spine. She should have remembered what it was like to provoke Flannigan. She saw the sparks come into the center of his eyes, saw the muscle tighten in his jaw, saw the tensing of his shoulders. But she wasn't about to back down. It was already too late.

"Yes, I said dull. I noticed it the minute I set eyes on you." He was out of his chair now. Adrenaline pumped through her, and she felt more alive than she had in years. "What a pity you've lost all your excitement."

He threw back his head and laughed. Then he leaned down and scooped her out of her chair. Her robe slid off her shoulders and landed on the floor. She lifted her gaze to his, and for a heartbeat she thought she'd been hurled back in time. Her lips parted.

Flannigan knew temptation. Tess was still firm where she should be, and soft in all the right places. She was like an armful of camellias, creamy and satiny and fragrant. He leaned so close, he was almost touching her lips.

"Do you think I'm going to kiss you, Tess, my girl?"

Her mouth snapped shut.

"It takes two to kiss, Flannigan. And I have no intention of kissing you."

"Good. Just so we understand each other."

He swung her over his shoulder, bottom up.

When she recovered her breath, she banged his back with her fists.

"What do you think you're doing? Put me down."

"Not until I get what I want."

He held her flailing legs still with one arm as he pulled off her left shoe.

"There now. That should do it."

He plunked her down unceremoniously onto her feet, and she stood in one shoe, lopsided, glowering at him. Now she knew how O'Toole had felt when she'd hauled him off the bed.

Flannigan held her shoe aloft, laughing. "Did you think I was going to kneel at your feet to get this?"

"I can never tell what you're going to do."

"You said I had grown dull with old age."

He reached for the bottle. A bright drop splashed onto the floor as he poured champagne into her shoe. Slowly, ever so slowly, he lifted her shoe toward his mouth. She couldn't take her eyes off his mouth—lush, warm, satiny. She knew just how it would feel.

"I was goading you," she said.

"Why?" He stared at her over the top of the shoe.

"I don't know." Suddenly she sat down and stared at the urn. "We always did bring out the worst in each other."

"And the best."

Tess watched as he tipped up her shoe and caught the sparkling champagne in his open mouth. One small drop wet his chin. She put her hand on the urn to keep from reaching up to wipe it off.

"Don't let me make a fool of myself, Babs," she whispered.

"Did you say something?"

"I said it was past time to go to bed."

The saints only knew why, but suddenly Mick wanted to prolong their time together in the kitchen.

"You didn't drink your champagne," he said.

"So I didn't."

Tess picked up her champagne and finished it off without lowering the glass. She wanted to be out of the kitchen, away from Mick Flannigan, but she'd die before she'd let him know that. Instead of retreating, she poured herself another glass.

"Toast, Flannigan." She held her glass aloft.

"Toast." He held out her shoe and clinked it against the rim of her glass.

"To Babs," she said.

"To the good old days."

They drank, their gazes locked.

"She used to say nobody else in the world could satisfy you except me. Remember that, Tess?"

"She was wrong." Tess swung her head toward the urn. "Sorry about that, Babs."

"So am I . . . extraordinarily sorry." Flannigan pulled a handkerchief from his pocket and wiped Tess's shoe. Then he knelt down and slipped it on her foot. "You still wear your dancing shoes wherever you go."

"Some things don't change, Flannigan." She steadied herself against the pleasure generated by his hand on her leg.

"You're right." He circled his hand slowly on her leg before letting her go. "Some things never change."

He stood up then, and she caught a glimpse of the little boy lost she'd known so many years before. He'd been tough and strong and wild, but every now and then his guard would slip and she'd see a bewildered child peering out from his blue eyes. Now, seeing that look again, she melted.

"Still chasing rainbows, Mick?"

"Always. It seems to me that the big one is just over the next hill."

"Where was your last hill?"

"Down in South America. I've been running a little flying school."

"Sounds exciting."

"I've always craved excitement. I guess it's my carnival upbringing."

"I think it's in your blood, Flannigan."

Tess caught his face between her hands and kissed him full on the lips. Then, with one hand still on his cheek, she whispered, "Someday I hope you find what you're looking for."

She left the kitchen swiftly, trailing ostrich plumes, the scent of jasmine, and a disgruntled cat. Mick was too stunned to tell her she'd forgotten Babs.

"I'll be damned."

He touched his hand to his lips and watched the empty kitchen doorway. It seemed Tess lingered there. That was the way it had always been with her. She stamped herself onto a place so that a part of her spirit was forever imprinted there. Everything she touched, even the very air she breathed, seemed permeated with her essence. That's why, after he had left her, he'd got rid of his belongings, one by one—the old battered suitcase she'd sometimes used in her out-of-town singing engagements; his favorite T-shirt she'd often worn while she hummed around the kitchen, burning hot dogs; his hairbrush with the few red strands of hair tangled in the bristles; his red wool socks she wore to bed in the winter when her feet got cold.

He reached for her glass and filled it with champagne.

"Here's to the past, Babs. I thought it was dead until I came here and saw her again."

Flannigan tipped up the glass and drained it in one single, smooth swallow. Then he refilled it, leaned back in his chair, and propped his bare feet on the table.

"Excuse me, Babs. A man likes to be comfortable when he drinks."

That's one of the things Uncle Arthur had taught him: Be comfortable when you drink. Good old Uncle Arthur. God rest his soul. The Incredible Fire-Breathing Man, finest attraction at the Brinkley Brothers' Carnival. Arthur wasn't really his uncle, of course. He didn't have any uncles. Or parents, either. No, he decided as he poured himself another drink, Mick Flannigan was a man alone, a man who knew how to move from place to place in order to find what he wanted.

When he was twelve years old, he'd merely wanted to be rid of the drab, structured life at the orphanage. So he'd run away, joined the carnival, taken up with Uncle Arthur. They'd more or less adopted each other. Then, when he'd left college, he'd been looking for the big score. He hadn't found it yet, just a series of small, unsatisfying scores, enough to keep body and soul together. And when he'd left Tess . . .

He held the glass high and inspected the golden liquid. What had he been searching for when he'd left Tess? Damned if he knew.

Even now, ten years later, he still didn't know what he was searching for. All he knew was that he had to keep searching. The siren song was playing, calling his name, wooing him, luring him over the next hill.

"Here's to the next hill . . . wherever it might be."

He sat in the kitchen until the bottle was empty. Then he stood up to go. His bare foot touched something soft and silky. Tess's robe. Looking down at the bit of herself she'd left behind, Mick smiled.

"You always did leave a trail, Tess." He scooped up the robe and held it against his face for a moment. Then he tossed it carelessly over his shoulder as if holding on to a part of Tess didn't matter anymore.

He put the bottle into the garbage can, picked up Babs, and left the kitchen. After he had carefully set the urn in its resting place, he climbed the stairs. His walk was sure and steady. Uncle Arthur had also taught him to hold his liquor.

He was halfway through his bedroom door before he changed his mind about going to bed. Pulling the silk robe off his shoulder, he smiled.

"Might as well return this to its rightful owner."

Three

Tess was spread across the bed like a fallen flower, her creamy gown glowing softly in the moonlight, her shoes still on her feet.

"Tess?" Flannigan stood in the doorway, softly calling her name, but he knew even as he did that she would not answer. Once Tess fell asleep, nothing less than a tornado could wake her.

He tiptoed into the room. Habit, he guessed. In his orphanage days he'd learned to tiptoe across a floor at night to keep from awakening a child who was dreaming of a home with real roses climbing on the white fence and real parents waiting beside the hearth. That had been his dream, too, when he was six years old. Fortunately for him, he'd got over that particular fantasy when he was about ten. He'd learned the hard way that it wouldn't happen, and never let himself wish for it again.

He approached the bed. At first he thought he'd drop the robe on the foot of her bed where she'd be sure to find it next morning; then he decided that he'd spread it over her. As usual she hadn't pulled up the covers, and he knew that when she woke up, even in the summertime, her feet would be cold—air conditioner cold now.

He sat down on the bed to spread the robe across her legs. She looked so silky, so soft. Without meaning to, he put one hand on her leg. He could feel the warmth of her skin through the gown.

Suddenly he was transported out of the bedroom in Tupelo, flung backward to a walk-up apartment in New York where the paint was peeling off the walls and the plumbing never worked right. He slid his hand down her leg, expecting any minute that she would turn over and reach for him, saying, "Flannigan, Flannigan," in a voice that always reminded him of music, even when she was drowsy.

"Ahhh, Tess, my girl. How could I ever have let you go?"

She didn't answer, of course. She slept on, just as she had ten years ago when he'd quietly packed his bags and walked out the door. Had it been an act of cowardice or an act of heroism? He didn't know then, and he didn't know now. At the time he'd believed he was making a great sacrifice for her sake. He had to be moving on, and it wouldn't be fair to uproot her when she was making a name for herself. She might have argued, of course. In fact, seeing her now, seeing the stubborn thrust of her chin even as she slept, he was certain that she would have argued. He had left without a word to avoid that argument. He'd propped a note on the nightstand and walked out the door and never looked back.

"Did your other husbands leave you, Tess?"

He couldn't imagine they would.

"Or did you send them packing?"

He hoped so. He hoped they were so inadequate

they couldn't possibly have satisfied a woman like Tess Jones Flannigan.

Funny how he automatically added his name to hers. He supposed that's what came from being with the group again, resurrecting old memories.

He spread the robe across her legs, smoothing it down and tucking it under her feet.

Tess stirred. Something was disturbing her dreams. Half awake, she was trapped by her dream in which she was running through her apartment, clutching a note in her hand, flinging open closet doors and kitchen cabinets. Looking for a toothbrush, a sock, a pair of wrinkled gym shorts—anything to tell her Flannigan had not left her. Then, suddenly, she felt his hand on her leg. She knew it was Flannigan, for his touch was like no other, exquisitely tender and thoroughly possessive at the same time.

"Mick?"

She sat up, rubbing sleep from her eyes. And there he was: sitting on the edge of her bed, looking delicious.

"You've come back."

She flung her arms around him and pressed her face into the warm hollow between his beard-stubbled cheek and his hard shoulder. Her tears wet his skin.

"Oh God, Mick. I thought you had gone. I thought you had left me."

She rained kisses along the side of his neck, across his shoulder. He gently cupped her face, tipping it up toward his.

"Ahh, Tess. . . " His eyes were shiny in the moonlight, and she knew he was crying too.

"I thought you didn't love me, Mick. I thought nobody loved me."

Lulled by memories and champagne, they came

together like two separate stars, destined to find their way back home across the sky. Her lips were sweet, and his were tender. Her embrace was warm, and his was safe. Her sighs were soft, and his were full of regret.

He kissed her knowing that he shouldn't, knowing that he'd had too much champagne and too much nostalgia. She kissed him with growing wonder, coming slowly out of her half-dreamy state, rising out of the fog of the past and landing in the middle of now.

Mick had not come back. She was in Tupelo in a strange bed and in the arms of her first husband. The first and the best, she thought as she kissed him. Flannigan had always been the best.

With her lips still on his she imagined the angels bending down to sigh with envy. Flannigan kissed with more than skill, more than expert knowledge; he kissed with his soul. She could feel his hopes and his dreams, his sadness and his disappointment, his strength and his joy, hovering just beyond the surface of his satiny-smooth and exquisitely possessive lips.

When they had to break apart for air, she opened her eyes and leaned her head back to look at him.

"Ahhh, Flannigan. How we could love."

He traced the graceful lines of her neck with the tips of his fingers.

"Don't think I'm not tempted, Tess." He bent down and skimmed his lips over her neck, bringing chill bumps to her skin. "I'm tempted to spread you across this bed and kiss every inch of your body." He lifted his head to look into her eyes. "Did you know that you're still the most sensational woman alive?"

"Yes." Her laughter was low and throaty.

"Always the invincible Tess Jones."

"Always."

She lied, of course. But she wasn't about to tell him the truth. Even when they were best friends, she'd kept part of herself secret from him. Like the rest of the world, he thought she was indestructible. That's what she wanted him to think. That's what she wanted them all to think.

Flannigan took one last taste of her skin, then he let her go. He stood up, and the mattress sprang back into place like a relieved toad that had been squashed under a rock.

"I can't say I'm sorry this happened, Tess."

"Neither can I."

She gazed up at him with her hair tumbling around her shoulders and one strap hanging so low, her gown barely covered her. Her eyes were the deep green of summer trees in the late evening. He'd have given a fortune to know what she was thinking. But he didn't have a fortune. And he didn't need to learn her thoughts again.

They were both merely passing through Tupelo. Chances were, after this weekend they wouldn't see each other again. And that's the way it should be. There was no going back.

He half-turned to go, but her voice stopped him.

"Why are you here . . . in my bedroom?"

"I was returning your robe. You left it in the kitchen."

"Thank you, Mick."

"You're welcome."

She stacked two pillows together and lay back on the bed, her arms laced behind her head.

"I lied to you earlier, Mick."

"When?"

"When I said you had lost your charm." She smiled. "You haven't."

"I knew that all along."

"But that doesn't mean this is going to happen again."

"You're right. It won't. I promise you."

She felt deflated, as if she were a party balloon and someone had maliciously stuck a pin in her and let out all her air. He didn't have to be so damned positive about the whole thing. Why was he so cool all of a sudden? Did he have another woman down in South America? Some hot Latin number who made him turn poetic in bed? Or maybe he had two or three women waiting for him. One in every port.

She didn't even want to think about that.

"You can leave now," she said. "And don't forget to close the door on your way out."

He left. The door had closed behind him with a muted sound of finality, she thought.

"He didn't even say good night," she told O'Toole.

O'Toole looked up from his comfortable spot on the needlepoint cushion of a small rocking chair. He yawned, showing his pointy teeth and his pink tongue. Then he turned his back to her, curled into a ball, and pretended to be asleep.

Tess knew better. That cagey cat just didn't want to be disturbed anymore.

All her life she had been disturbing people. First Aunt Bertha, who had taken over the job of bringing up two little girls when their mother had died. Tess had been twelve, and already too much a hellion to tame. At least, that's what Aunt Bertha kept telling her. Her sister, Margaret Leigh, was always the quiet one, the obedient one. But Tess spent most of her waking moments thinking of ways to break all the rules Aunt Bertha laid down.

At fourteen she'd snitched a pack of Lucky Strikes from Grandpa Jones and smoked behind the barn, standing defiantly with her legs apart and a hand on her hip, just because Aunt Bertha had said that real ladies didn't smoke standing up. Real ladies didn't cuss, either. Tess had used some doozies just to get Aunt Bertha's dander up. Or perhaps to get her attention.

Tess lay back against the pillows and mulled that over. Margaret Leigh had always been loved because she was nice and obedient; but Aunt Bertha spent most of her time trying to change Tess. So did everybody else: her relatives, her teachers, even her many husbands. Well, not all of them. Flannigan never had. He'd simply left her. But the other two—Carson and O'Toole—had set about trying to remake her the minute the first flush of honeymoon bliss was over.

"If you straighten up, Tess," they'd say, "you might *really* amount to something someday."

She hadn't necessarily wanted to amount to something, especially not something that everybody else decided she should be. She only wanted to be loved for herself.

She'd never said that to a living soul, not even Mick. To the rest of the world she was bold and wild and flamboyant and indestructible. And most of the time, it was true. But sometimes, when the night wind moaned against the windowpanes and the pillow next to hers didn't have so much as a tiny dent, and even her cat ignored her, Tess was not any of those things. She was fragile and vulnerable and so lonesome that all the blues songs she'd ever sung couldn't express the depth of her aloneness.

"Tess Jones," she told herself firmly, "if you don't stop pitying yourself, you'll never get to sleep and then you'll be too pooped to party."

She resolutely scrunched under the covers and shut her eyes.

The next morning, when the sun was high in the sky and everyone in the group had assembled, all dressed in comfortable summer clothes, they went on a picnic. It was reminiscent of all the picnics they'd ever taken together. And they took the urn.

Jim carried the hamper, piled high with food; Lovey carried the blankets to spread on the ground; Mick brought the ice chest, filled with an assortment of sandwiches and soft drinks and a chocolate cake Tess had insisted on; Tess brought the fireworks; and Johnny brought Babs, holding her carefully as they all jammed into his station wagon, laughing and trying to beat each other to the window seats.

"You drive," Johnny told Mick.

"But not like you used to," Lovey added, "all hell-bent for leather. I don't want to have this baby before its time."

Tess purposely sat on the backseat, as far away from Mick as she could get. He had said last night wouldn't happen again, but seeing him this morning, she wasn't so sure about it. All the things that had attracted her to him so many years before were still there: his big laugh, his easy smile, his teasing eyes, his humorous viewpoint, his passion.

Heaven help her. Passion simply oozed from the man's pores. In some ways she'd be glad when the weekend was over.

In deference to Lovey's wishes Mick drove sedately to City Park on Joyner Avenue.

"Hey, look at that." Jim studied the park out the window as Mick eased into the parking lot. "This place hasn't changed since we all came up for Johnny and Babs's wedding. Same old swingsets."

"The seesaw is what I want," Tess said.

"It takes two." Mick caught her eye in the rearview mirror.

"I know. I'm going to put Lovey on the other end so I can ride high."

While everyone else laughed, Tess stared back at Mick in the mirror, not willing to be the first to look away.

"Are you implying I'm fat?" Lovey patted her stomach.

"I don't want to hurt your feelings, Lovey. But it's a fact."

"It's all Jim's fault."

Everybody laughed once more. But underneath the laughter there was a sense of wonder. Each person in the car felt it. Journeys ended and journeys began. The cycle repeated itself, over and over. Babs had already embarked upon a mysterious voyage to another realm, while a tiny being awaited his turn to journey into the world.

Looking at Flannigan's profile in the rearview mirror, Tess decided that all of life was a journey. Even marriage. With Flannigan, she'd thought the journey would last forever. But it hadn't. He'd got off somewhere along the line. She'd gone on, though, picked up another partner and continued. To what? Happiness? Not really. Happiness didn't seem to be a place you could arrive at, like some distant spot on the map. Happiness seemed to be something that sprang to life involuntarily, like violets growing wild in an unexpected place.

At the moment Tess was happy. The sun was shining, the picnic hamper was full, and her friends were at her side.

"Hey, everybody," she yelled, "are we going to just sit in the car or what?"

"Or what!" Jim opened the door, and they began to pile out. Mick came last, laughing the loudest, talking the most. And yet, somehow he managed to avoid being in direct contact with Tess.

She noticed. She told herself it was wise. She told herself it shouldn't hurt. But it did.

The picnic was just like ones in the old days. Five of them now, they raced with boiled eggs in a spoon, they seesawed, they played tennis, they ate more than they should have, and they talked and talked. Through it all, Tess and Flannigan gave each other a wide berth, not so wide that the others noticed, but wide, nonetheless.

When dusk came, Lovey and Jim carried a blanket to a quiet spot so she could rest before the fireworks; Johnny took the urn and went for a long walk, and suddenly Tess and Flannigan were alone.

He sat on one end of a redwood bench under a spreading oak tree and Tess sat at the other. The grove was alive with nature's creatures who had come out to play. A small bunny hopped out of the undergrowth and sat nearby, munching tender green leaves. Cricket song echoed on the breeze that had sprung up with the darkness, and a string of fireflies hovered over a young pine, decorating its branches with blinking yellow lights.

Tess and Flannigan watched the evening display in silence for a while, strangely disturbed by their sudden isolation from the rest of the group. Finally he spoke.

"This is not by design."

"I know. I don't want to be alone with you anymore than you want to be alone with me."

The sting of that remark took him completely by surprise. He scooted across the bench until he was sitting by her side.

"Don't take this personally," he said. "It just occurred to me that the others might get the wrong idea if we keep sitting so far apart."

"What wrong idea would that be?"

"That we have a reason . . . that we're afraid of getting too close to each other again."

"That's ridiculous." She moved closer to him so that their thighs and shoulders were touching. "Just because we were once husband and wife is no reason we can't still be friends."

"Right." He was glad the darkness covered his smile, because he knew it was smug. Though why in the hell he should be smug about sitting beside a woman he had no intention of getting involved with again was beyond him. And he didn't intend to rationalize. He was feeling mellow, and she was, after all, an old friend, and that was that.

"So, tell me, Tess . . ." He turned to look into her eyes. That was a mistake. He'd forgotten how appealing Tess was in the last light of evening. Everything about her was softened—her blazing hair, her vivid coloring, her bright eyes. He lifted his hand toward her cheek, then he remembered touching her was taboo. "Mosquitoes," he said as he waved his hand around in the air.

She grinned. Dammit, she'd probably seen through him. To make matters worse, he'd forgotten what he had been going to say.

"What were you about to ask me to tell you, Flannigan?"

"Have you picked out husband number four?"

She lost her softness. Her rigid body spoke a language all its own, one he understood too well. But it was too late for him to call back his teasing words.

"Have I picked out husband number four?" Her words were carefully spaced as she turned full around and pinned him with her eyes. "Did I hear you correctly, Flannigan?"

His own temper flared. What did she want from

him? Congratulations on her many marriages? He was only human.

"You heard me correctly."

"Am I to take it that you're interested in my state of affairs, or is this idle curiosity?"

"Hell, Tess. We were married once."

"What's that supposed to mean? Just because you were husband number one doesn't give you any rights—"

"Husband number one!" He was getting madder by the minute.

So was she. Leaning so close her nose was touching his, she yelled in his face.

"If you'll recall, you were the one who did the walking. Not me."

"It wasn't like that, Tess."

"Like hell! You left a *note*, Flannigan. A lousy note."

"I knew you wouldn't understand. That's the reason I never talked to you about it."

"You didn't give me a chance to understand, you no-account philandering bum."

"Philandering!" His voice thundered through the grove, sending the rabbit into flight. And then it dropped to the soft silky tone that signaled real trouble. "Did you say philandering?"

Tess knew what was coming, but she wouldn't have quivered in her boots even if she'd been wearing them. This was a quarrel that had waited ten years to happen. She'd saved up ten years of questions and heartbreak and anger. And now she was going to let it all loose.

"That's what I said, Flannigan."

"Don't you know"—his hands gripped her shoulders, and his face grew savage—"*Don't you know, Tess?*" He bent so close, his lips were nearly on hers. "There was never another woman. Never has been. You were the only woman for me. Always were and always—" *God, in heaven. What are you saying, Flannigan?*

He claimed her mouth in a kiss that sizzled the hair along the back of his neck. *And you always will be, Tess. Always.* The clarity of his vision rocked him. He didn't know how to handle the revelation except to keep on kissing.

Her response was mind-bending. Anger had always made her kisses fierce. The madder she was, the hotter her kisses. He thought he and Tess would set the park on fire. That would be just as well, for what happened between them could never be anything more than a flash fire.

Tess molded herself to the body she knew so well. Out of habit, she told herself as the kiss went on and on. First love was not easily forgotten. And it certainly wasn't easily ignored, especially when her first lover was sitting beside her in the soft darkness of a summer evening, holding her as if she were the most precious thing in the world.

Ahhh, she wanted his kiss, needed his kiss. For just a moment it seemed as if the curtain of time was lifted and they were once again young lovers, traveling together into the future.

He shifted, and she was suddenly on his lap. How easy it was, sliding onto Flannigan's lap, as if they had done the same thing only yesterday.

The kiss climbed and climbed until it was up among the stars where kissing wasn't enough. He put one hand on the front of her blouse, on her buttons.

"Ahh, Tess. It was always this way with us."

The sound of his voice brought her back from the misty realms of the past, back to the park bench, back to Tess Jones who had long ago been divorced from him. He was just passing through her life again. She had to let him pass through, for she couldn't bear being hurt by him all over again.

Panting, she shoved hard against his chest, and slid off his lap and onto the end of the bench.

"Do you think it's that easy, Flannigan? Do you think all you have to do is crook your little finger and I'll walk back into your life?"

The world shifted into place for Flannigan, too, and he knew he had been close to making a terrible mistake.

"I don't want you back in my life."

"Well, you certainly gave a good imitation of wanting me back in your bed."

"That sounds tempting . . . but no, I don't even want you there, Tess."

"Then *why*?" She spread held her hands palm up in supplication. "Why did you kiss that way?"

"You kissed back."

"Dammit, Flannigan." She ran her hands through her hair, feeling the dampness that always collected on her scalp when she came this far south, where the humidity was so thick she could almost taste it.

"All right. I admit it. I kissed you back." She lifted her hair off her neck. "You were always a good kisser. And you know how much I like kissing. I never could resist it."

He didn't answer her right away, but lit a cigar and watched her over its glowing tip. She fanned herself with her hand.

"Tess, I don't plan to get started with you again."

"You're safe. You had one chance, Flannigan. You won't get another."

They stared at each other in the darkness lit with the glow of fireflies, and both of them remembered that first chance, remembered and wept inside.

Suddenly Mick cocked his head, listening.

"Did you hear something, Tess?"

"No."

"I thought I heard something back there in the trees. Just my imagination, I guess." He paused to blow smoke rings and watch them mingle with the glow of fireflies. Then he turned back to Tess. "I think I owe you something."

"What?"

"An explanation."

"It won't change things."

"No, it won't. But it might ease my conscience. It's been giving me the devil because I left you without an explanation."

"Good. I hope it pained you something fierce."

"It did. Especially the first two days."

"Two days! Only two days, Flannigan? It took me two weeks to get over you."

"You'll notice I wasn't the one who rushed into the arms of somebody else."

"I didn't rush. I sort of meandered. I lived with Carson two years before I married him. And with O'Toole—"

"Hell, Tess. . . "

"They didn't last. Just like you."

"The fools left you?"

"No. I sent them packing."

"Good."

"Why? Why could it possibly matter to you whether I sent them away?"

"Because you deserve the best."

She looked out across the grove, the expression on her face dreamy.

"I had the best . . . once."

They sat side by side, not touching, both facing forward, as if they were on a train together going somewhere, both planning to get off at different stops. They were still and thoughtful for so long, the rabbit got brave and came back into the grove.

Tess broke the silence.

"Your note said, 'I'm sorry I have to go. Love, Mick.' Why did you sign it 'Love Mick'?"

"Because it was true. That's the reason I left . . . because I loved you."

She hopped off the bench and faced him, furious, legs wide apart and hands on her hips.

"You loved me enough to leave me while I was sleeping, without even saying good-bye, without even telling me why you were going or where? That's not love, Flannigan. That's selfishness."

"You're right. I was selfish. But still, I loved you."

She turned and stomped away, but he ground his cigar under his boot and caught up to her. With his hands on her shoulders he turned her around to face him. She was rigid with rage.

"I don't blame you for being mad, Tess."

"Mad doesn't begin to describe what I felt after I got over being hurt. I wanted to kill you, Flannigan."

His grin was rueful. "It looks like you still do."

"I wouldn't waste my time."

"Ahh, Tess . . . Tess, my girl." His thumbs caressed her shoulders. They were hot from a day in the sun.

"I left because I had to go and I couldn't take you with me."

"Why not, I'd like to know? I was your wife."

"And you'd have gone out of loyalty."

"I'd have gone out of love. Dammit, I loved you, Mick Flannigan."

"It wouldn't have been fair, Tess . . . dragging you all over creation while I chased rainbows . . . the rainbows I promised myself in the orphanage that I was going to chase."

"Leaving me behind was fair, Mick?"

Suddenly she was mellow and soft again. When Flannigan looked down at her with his expression tender and his eyes the color of a summer day, she couldn't stay mad at him. No matter what he had done.

"Maybe not, Tess . . ." He circled his thumbs on her skin one last time, and then he let her go. "Maybe it wasn't fair, but it was the only thing I could do."

He walked away. She kicked at a stick on the ground. Tears formed in her eyes, but she pressed the heel of hands against them.

"Dammit. I cried for you once, Mick Flannigan. I'll never cry for you again. Never."

She went back to the bench and sat down again. The faint odor of his cigar still lingered in the air. She reached down and picked up its remains.

"I found one of these the last time you left. A half-smoked cigar. Some going-away present."

She brooded over the cigar for so long, a firefly settled on her arm. She looked down at the small bug. Its wings were folded over a small black-and-orange body, and its taillight was turned off. She could see the yellow bottom, resting against her skin.

"They say if a firefly lights on you, it's good luck."

It soared away, blinking its light once more in the darkness.

"I always did believe in luck." She still held the cigar in her hand. With a flick of her wrist she tossed it onto the ground. "But not the Mick Flannigan kind of luck."

She left the bench and went to find Jim and Lovey.

From his hiding place behind a nearby tree an old man watched her go. He'd been watching and listening for some time, long enough to know exactly what was going on between Tess and Flannigan.

As soon as she was out of hearing range, he started singing softly to himself, "In the sweet by and by, we will meet on that beautiful shore."

When Tess was out of sight, his voice trailed off and he chuckled.

"Well, now," he announced to the trees, "I hope that lightning bug brings her some luck."

Four

Flannigan was in charge of the fireworks.

Tess sat on the blanket with Lovey and Jim, watching him and thinking how appropriate that he was the one lighting Roman candles and sending them blazing into the sky, streaming bright trails of red and yellow and green. Flannigan had always been in charge of fireworks—of all kinds, she thought wryly.

She tried to keep her mind off the most recent fireworks on the park bench and heaved a big sigh. She had almost let things get out of control.

"What's the matter, Tess?" Lovey turned to her.

"I guess I'm just feeling blue."

"Me too. Even if we did say this was going to be a going-away party for Babs, I can't help but feel sad and lonesome. I miss her."

"So do I."

Tess felt guilty. Her sadness wasn't so much for Babs as for herself. It seemed that she was losing Mick all over again.

That didn't make any sense, of course. But she'd forgive herself if she appeared a little foolish. A woman wasn't supposed to be sane and rational when her best friend was ashes and her first husband was a lion, the great savage kind that kept stalking her, coming out of the bushes at unexpected times and circling her until he was ready to come in for the kill.

She shivered.

"I know." Lovey reached over and squeezed Tess's hand. "That's how I feel too. Sort of chilled down to the soul."

Tess let herself be consoled. After all, the touch of a friend wasn't a gift to be taken lightly.

After the fireworks they gathered their picnic items and headed home, more somber than when they'd arrived. Flannigan drove again. Tess somehow ended up on the front seat, squashed so tightly between Mick and John that she couldn't tell where she left off and they began. Johnny's legs, she didn't mind. They were just legs. But Flannigan's! They weren't legs, they were more fireworks, more Roman candles—these going off under her skin.

Flannigan didn't seem to notice. His hands were loose and relaxed on the wheel, and he turned his head from time to time, leaning a bit so he could see around her, talking to Johnny. She had no idea what they were talking about. It didn't concern her. Nothing concerned her except getting out of the car.

They finally got back to Johnny's house. After they had unloaded, they all went their separate ways to wash the day's grime and dust away before getting back together for dinner.

Johnny had ordered Chinese food. It was set up on trays around the den. So was the movie projector. He was quite a camera buff, and had never gone anywhere without a good camera in his hand.

Perched on the piano bench across the room from Tess, Flannigan watched reel after reel of captured memories of their college days. There was Tess, running barefoot across the campus, waving a test paper and shouting. When she got close enough, they all heard what she was shouting.

"That old fogy! Why do they call it creative writing if you're not supposed to be creative?"

Everybody in the den laughed, just as they had laughed that day. Tess had written a jazzy story about picking locks.

"Well, he said he wanted a how-to story," the young Tess on the film said. "How did I know he wanted something stuffy, like how to sew on a button."

Johnny paused the film and called across the room to Tess. She was sitting on a pile of red cushions, her legs tucked under.

"Hey, Tess. Who's sewing on your buttons now?"

"I'm looking, Johnny. I haven't found him yet, but I will."

She didn't even glance Flannigan's way. He reached for a cigar and crammed it into his mouth unlit. He needed something to bite, preferably something that wouldn't scream.

Johnny started the film again, and there they were, at the graduation dance. Lovey and Jim, gazing fondly into each other's eyes. Babs blowing a kiss into the camera. Tess and Flannigan, dancing cheek to cheek.

He bit into his cold cigar again. Lord, he remembered how it had felt to dance with her. Like floating. Her body pressed so close to his, he could feel her heart pounding against his chest. Her arms wrapped around his neck, one hand making circles on his skin and the other laced in his hair.

The film had captured it all. He wanted to look across the room. He wanted to see her face, but he dared not. Instead he clamped the cigar between his teeth and stared at the screen.

The dance went on and on, until Flannigan thought he'd bite his cigar in half. The next reel wasn't any better for his peace of mind. Johnny had filmed the group at Lake Tiak-O'khata with the girls cavorting in the sunshine, eating snow cones with juice dripping down their chins and making purple trails into the tops of their bikinis. Tess filled his senses just as she filled the screen. He could see no one but Tess.

If he could have left the room without hurting Johnny's feeling, he would have. But he couldn't let his old friend down, even if it was killing him to sit there and watch Tess and remember how it had been between them.

Dear Lord, the way they had loved in the back of his old hearse. And laughed. He could close his eyes and still hear the sound of her laughter, sometimes low and throaty and other times high and trilling, like silver bells ringing on a Sunday morning.

He closed his eyes, blessedly blocking out her image. Still he could hear her laughter, echoing back from their past. Tomorrow they would all fly into the sky and scatter Babs's ashes, and then they'd go their separate ways. Tess would go back to her career in Chicago, and he'd go . . . the saints only knew where.

It was after midnight when the home movies ended and the group said good night.

Tess was the first to go. Flannigan figured she couldn't wait to be rid of him. He felt the same way about her. But probably not for the same reasons. He wanted to get on his hands and knees at her feet and beg her forgiveness. He wanted to call back time, and undo everything he had done to the woman he'd loved most in the world. The only woman he'd ever love. If he could call back time, he would start making amends by undoing their marriage. It had been selfish of him to pledge vows when he didn't even know who in the hell he was and what he wanted from life.

It was too bad that wisdom didn't come with youth but arrived when it was much too late, like a Christmas package lost in the mail until June. Flannigan sat in his chair, smoking his cigar, thinking his wise thoughts, and watching his friends leave the room.

In deference to Lovey's condition Jim carried his wife up the stairs, struggling a little under her weight.

Johnny picked up the urn, then turned to Flannigan.

"Coming, Mick?"

"Not yet."

"It got to you, didn't it?"

"What?"

"Seeing the way it used it to be with you and Tess."

Mick couldn't lie to an old friend. "Some," he said. "But I'll get over it."

"Maybe you shouldn't try." Johnny hugged the urn to his chest. "I know this is trite, but life is short, too short to waste time alone if you love somebody." His smile was sad. "Do you still love her, Mick?"

"I never stopped."

"Then go to her. Nothing would please me more

than to know that Babs's last gift to you and Tess was getting you two back together."

"It's not that simple, Johnny."

"Hell, I know that." Johnny sighed. "I guess I'm just feeling sentimental and sad . . . sad for myself and Babs, even sad for you and Tess." He caught Mick's shoulder and squeezed. "Good night, Mick."

Johnny didn't stop by the hall table but went up the staircase, holding Babs over his heart. Mick's eyes suddenly felt hot, and he blinked away the tears. Then he slipped through the house and out the back door into the garden, fragrant with summer flowers.

He leaned against the trunk of a huge magnolia tree and lit his cigar. Then he gazed up at Tess's window. He could see her silhouette against the drawn shade. It appeared briefly, then vanished, then reappeared. The pattern repeated itself over and over. She was pacing.

He wondered if he were the cause of her restlessness, just as she was the cause of his.

He stayed in the darkness, gazing up at her window until she extinguished the light and went to bed.

"Think of me, Tess . . . Think of me with kindness."

He left the dark night shade of the lush magnolia and sat in a willow glider, swinging gently back and forth. The cigar burned down to the tips of his fingers, and still he sat in the swing.

Suddenly lights began to spring on all over the house. Good Lord. Something was wrong. Flannigan tossed the butt of his cigar onto the ground and began to run. What if something had happened to Tess? It had to be Tess, for she was the only one who'd be up prowling around in the middle of the night. And she was never careful about anything. Always headlong and high-strung.

His mind raced as fast as his feet. What if Tess had tripped and fallen down the stairs? She was always trailing things behind her. All those damned feathers.

He flung open the back door, but the kitchen was still dark, and he couldn't see a thing. He could hear footsteps and people calling back and forth upstairs.

"Tess," he roared. "Tess!"

She appeared at the head of the staircase, dragging her purple peignoir behind her. Relief surged through him, and on its heels, anger.

"Put that damned thing on before you step on it and kill yourself," he yelled, taking the steps two at a time.

"What is the matter with you?" She rammed one arm into the sleeve just as he reached the top of the staircase. "Have you gone mad?"

He didn't answer, but jerked the peignoir around her shoulders and crammed in her other arm.

"What are you doing?"

"Taking care of you."

"I've been taking of myself for ten years. I don't need any help now."

"It seems to me that you do, tromping around the house at the damndest hours, drinking champagne, wearing all these feathers." He drew her peignoir high around her neck and held her that way, glaring down at her. "If you don't smother to death in all these feathers, you're going to get tangled up and trip down the stairs and kill yourself."

"Turn my feathers loose."

He suddenly realized how ridiculous he was

being. With Tess around, things always got magnified.

"Hell." He released her and stepped back.

"Tess!" Johnny yelled, sticking his head around Lovey's bedroom door. "Hurry up. I need you." Then he vanished.

"What's going on?" Flannigan asked.

"Lovey's having her baby. Don't just stand there with your mouth open. Make yourself useful."

"What do you want me to do?"

"For one thing, you can keep Jim out of the way so Johnny and I can deliver that baby. He's driving us all crazy."

Tess disappeared into Lovey's bedroom, and Jim came out. His hair and eyes were wild, and he was feeling the walls like a blind man.

Mick took his arm and led him to the staircase.

"Everything's going to be all right, Jim."

Jim sank onto the top step. "It's too early, Mick. The baby's not due for at least two weeks."

"Johnny's a doctor. He'll take care of Lovey."

"It all happened so quickly. There wasn't even time to get her to a hospital. What if something happens to Lovey and the baby?"

"Relax, Jim. They'll be fine."

Jim sat rigid on the staircase, and Mick wasn't much better. A baby, he thought. Saints be praised. A baby being born right here in this house. And Tess in there helping to deliver it. He got misty-eyed thinking about Tess bringing a baby into the world.

Time stretched out while they waited; thirty minutes seemed like three hours. Then Johnny appeared in Lovey's bedroom doorway.

"You can go in now, Jim. You have a beautiful, healthy baby girl. Lovey's fine." Johnny held the door wide. "Why don't you come, too, Mick?"

Mick trailed along behind, not certain he wanted

to be a part of this intimate family gathering. He changed his mind the minute he entered the bedroom.

Tess was standing beside the bed, holding the baby. She was bending close so her hair made a bright curtain behind the baby's head. One tiny hand was wrapped around Tess's finger, and her smile was so tender and shining, Mick decided the angels had touched her face with glory.

Tess and the baby were the most beautiful picture Mick had ever seen. He didn't even bother to wipe the tears from his eyes as he leaned against the doorframe, watching her.

Tess looked up, directly at Mick. Although she was still smiling, her own eyes were bright, and Mick thought he saw a glimmer of tears on her cheeks.

"Come and see her," Tess said softly. "She's beautiful."

Mick tiptoed across the room. At that moment Tess loved him all over again. He looked so heartbreakingly innocent, a large, rowdy man trying to be as quiet as possible. When he reached her and put his big hand on the baby's tiny cheek, Tess thought she would cry. *Really* cry. Not the quiet sniffling that ladies did, but the loud, red-nosed, red-eyed, lusty bawling of true heartbreak.

"She's so *small*," Mick whispered.

Jim, who was sitting on the edge of the bed holding Lovey's hand, looked up and laughed. "They grow."

Johnny came back into the room with the urn and stood at the foot of Lovey's bed.

"We have something we want to tell all of you," said Lovey, squeezing her husband's hand. "Will you hand me the baby, Tess?"

Tess bent over the bed and placed the small

bundle in Lovey's arms. The baby opened her rosebud mouth in a yawn and batted the air with one tiny fist.

"Through the years," Lovey said, "this circle of friends has been more important to us than wealth or possessions or prestige. Friendship is a gift of the heart. It's a spontaneous caring and sharing that grows more precious as the years go by." Lovey paused, smiling down at her new baby; then she lifted her head and smiled at her friends. "One of our circle has begun a journey that has to be made alone. In honor and memory of her, we want to name this baby Babs."

Mick caught Tess's hand and she caught Johnny's and he caught Jim's and Jim squeezed Lovey's. The circle was complete.

"I'm overwhelmed," said Johnny, fighting back tears. "I can't think of anything that would have pleased Babs more."

Johnny and Tess and Mick admired the baby, then stole quietly from the room. Johnny disappeared into his bedroom, carrying the urn. Mick and Tess stood facing each other in the hallway.

"I don't think I can sleep after this," she whispered.

"I wasn't sleeping anyway." Mick took her elbow and led her downstairs to the kitchen. Then he pulled out a chair for Tess and began to rummage in the cabinets. "Scotch," he said, holding the bottle and turning so Tess could see. "A man's drink. Do you want some."

"Why not?"

Mick poured two drinks and sat down beside her. They drank in silence for a while, watching each other over the rims of their glasses.

"I can't get my mind off that baby," Tess said.

"Neither can I."

"She is so perfect."

"As fair as the first flowers of spring."

"That's beautiful, Mick."

They lapsed into silence once more, this time careful to keep from looking at each other. When their glasses were empty, Mick refilled them.

"We were going to have children, Tess. You and I."

"It's not my fault we didn't. You're the one who left."

"Back to that again, are we?"

"And why not? I'll have you know, Mick Flannigan, that there are some things a woman can't do alone."

"That's quite an admission coming from you, Tess Flannigan."

"That's not my name."

"Pardon me. Tess Jones Flannigan Carson O'Toole. Did I leave anybody out?"

Their tempers had flared as quickly as their passion always did. Their chairs were scooted closer together now, and they glared at each other, nose to nose.

Tess set her glass on the table without ever breaking eye contact with Flannigan.

"Flannigan, sometimes you're a bastard."

"Correct." His glass rattled as he set it on the table. "I never knew my mother, God rest her soul, and I don't even know if I had a daddy. I was probably spawned by the devil. That would be quite a heritage for a kid, wouldn't it?"

"Oh God, Mick." She could have wept. Instead she reached out and tenderly touched his cheek. "I'm sorry."

He covered her hand with his own. "How many times are we going to say that before this weekend is over?"

"I don't know. It seems that you and I always create the *need* to say it. Why is that, Mick?"

"Ahhh . . . Tess." He pressed their joined hands closer against her cheek and held them there while crickets serenaded the night and the moon tracked across the sky.

Flannigan and Tess searched each other's eyes for the truth, but it kept darting out of their sight. Finally he leaned down and pressed a tender kiss on her forehead.

"For all the ways I've hurt you, I'm truly sorry, Tess, my girl."

"We were so young," she whispered. "So young."

"And very much in love."

"Yes. That too."

He lifted her into his arms, and she leaned her head against his chest. It felt so good, she thought, so right to be held this way by him.

"I'm taking you up to bed, Tess. You're tired."

"Thank you."

She reached out and flicked off the light as they passed through the kitchen doorway.

"Can you see in the dark, Mick?"

"I have a flame to light the way—your hair." He leaned down and pressed his face in her hair. "It's beautiful in the moonlight."

They passed silently through the den toward the staircase; then he started the long climb to the top. His boots made a muffled cadence on the carpeted stairs, keeping time with the beat of her heart. She didn't know where he was taking her—to her bedroom or to his. It didn't matter. Not tonight. Destiny had brought them to Tupelo, and chance had put her in his arms. If it hadn't been for the baby and the scotch and the past, they might not be on this particular staircase with the moon lighting their way to the top.

Tess closed her eyes and pressed her face into the front of his shirt. All the wonderful fragrances of the day were mingled in his clothes—the scent of grass where he'd sprawled with his pimiento sandwich, the essence of chocolate where he'd dropped a crumb of cake, the sweet smoky smell of his cigar, even the sharp, bright smell of sunshine seemed to be hidden deep within Mick Flannigan.

At the top of the stairs Mick hesitated. Then he headed resolutely toward Tess's door. He carried her into the bedroom and kicked the door shut with his boot.

"Here we are, Tess."

She opened her eyes. The moon was streaming across the bed.

"Do you remember the first time we ever made love, Flannigan?"

"I could never forget."

"The moon was shining, just like tonight."

"It was summer," he said.

"You were scared."

"I was bold. You were scared."

"I was pretending. I didn't want you to think I was an easy girl."

He chuckled softly. "You were never easy, but you were always wicked."

"That's part of my charm."

"So it is, Tess, my girl."

He started toward the bed, then stopped in the middle of the room, gazing down at her. She put both hands on his cheeks.

"Kiss me, Flannigan. One more time."

"Once was never enough for us, Tess."

Time stood still as he lowered his mouth to hers. Their lips touched, and they knew what heaven was like. She clung to his shoulders, and he held her against his heart. He slid one hand into her hair, and she slipped her hand under the back of his shirt. Her hair was fragrant, and his skin was warm.

"Tess . . . my Tess," he whispered against her lips.

"Flannigan . . . my love."

Her fingertips raked his skin, and he shuddered.

"You are almost more temptation than a man can bear. You bewitch me, Tess."

"You're worth the price of sorcery."

Their lips joined once more, and they clung together, tasting the nectar of the gods. Then, slowly, resolutely, he started toward the bed.

Five

The mattress sagged under their weight. Flannigan spread her across the bed, just the way he used to, with her hair fanning brightly on the pillow and her silky gown smoothed down so her body made one long, lithe line in the moonlight, uninterrupted by wrinkles. Propped on one knee, he leaned over her, his hand warm on her thigh.

"When I see you like this, Tess, I call myself a fool."

"You never were. Only scared." She traced the arch of his eyebrows, the shape of his cheekbone, the fine outline of his full lips.

"That feels good." Closing his eyes, he sighed. "I could fall asleep right here, lying next to you on this mattress with your hands on my face."

"*Sleep*, Flannigan?"

"Among other things."

He stayed where he was awhile longer, with his hand on her leg and her hand on his face. He felt selfish, taking so much pleasure and knowing he couldn't give any in return. But he felt noble too. It wasn't often a man was called upon to leave the bed of a woman like Tess.

"You tempt me to stay, Tess."

"You tempt me to invite you."

Abruptly he stood, before he changed his mind. Looking down at her, he gave a sad, wistful smile.

"I could never hurt you again, Tess. You're too important to me."

"I suppose I should thank you for that." She reached out for a second pillow, and propped herself up so she could see him better. "Instead I'll ask for one last favor."

"Name it. It's yours."

"Kiss me good night, Flannigan, and then go quickly."

He bent over her and tenderly cupped her face. Then he gave her a kiss that started music in her soul. It was tender and sweet and endearing. And it was good-bye. She could feel the loneliness of parting, even as they clung to each other.

At last he broke away. Their eyes met briefly; then he turned quickly and left the room, as she had told him to. The door closed behind him, and she wished she had told him to stay. But what if he had? The loving would have magnificent; there was no doubt about that. They would have stayed in each other's arms all night long. But when morning came . . . what would happen then?

She tossed one of the pillows across the bed and lay down on the other. She was foolish to be wishing such things. Forgetting that her shoes were still on her feet, she drifted asleep.

The sounds of a baby crying woke Tess. She pushed her hair out of her face and peered at the bedside clock, but O'Toole had his tail curled over its face, so she had to shove him out of the way before she could see the dial.

Six o'clock. She hadn't been awake at six o'clock in the morning since she was fourteen and Aunt Bertha had rousted her out of bed to dress for school. "But it's *two hours* before school," she'd complain every morning. And Aunt Bertha would always say, "The early bird gets the worm." "But I don't *like* worms," she'd retort knowing full well that Aunt Bertha would tell her that real ladies didn't sass their elders.

Tess crumpled back onto the bed, preparing to fall asleep again, but the baby resumed crying. She was fully awake now. Funny how nothing less than a freight train could wake her when she was in Chicago, and now the small sound of a newborn baby brought her out of a deep slumber in Tupelo.

She slung her peignoir over her shoulders, found her shoes, which had come off during the night and were hidden under the covers, and cracked open Lovey's bedroom door. Lovey was sitting on the bed, holding the crying baby, and Jim was still sound asleep on the cot he'd pulled out of the hall closet the night before.

"Is anything wrong?" Tess asked.

"No. She's dry and fed, and this is not a cry of pain. I think she's lonesome. It seems to be the universal human condition." Lovey smiled at Tess and motioned her into the bedroom. "Come in and visit."

Tess tiptoed inside. Lovey patted the mattress beside her.

"Are you sure it's all right? I know we were all in here last night . . . but I've read about hospitals protecting babies from germs and that sort of thing."

"Isolation is a far greater threat than germs. Believe me. Jim and I both think that bonding far outweighs caution."

Tess sat on the edge of the bed, gazing down at the baby.

"She's so fragile. Aren't you afraid of hurting her?"

"As long as you keep them close to your body so they won't think they're falling and you're careful to support their little heads, babies do fine." She looked at the naked longing in Tess's face. "Do you want to hold her?"

"If you think it will be all right."

She arranged her arms stiffly, and Lovey placed the baby into them. Little Babs was still sniffling and making unhappy faces, and this new turn of events didn't cause her any great pleasure. She yelled louder.

"What do I do now?" Tess was genuinely alarmed.

"Why don't you try walking her and singing to her? Babies love the sound of the human voice."

Tess stood up and began to walk the baby, uneasily at first, and then, as she got the hang of it, with more confidence. She started humming too. An Irish lullaby she'd learned years ago when she and Flannigan were first dating.

The baby quieted immediately. With her little hand tangled in a long strand of Tess's red hair, she gazed at her latest source of entertainment.

"I think she likes me."

"She loves the sound of your voice. And who wouldn't, Tess? You still have the voice of an angel." Lovey leaned back against the pillows.

"You must be exhausted."

"More tired than I should be. It's my age, I guess. I was much younger when I had the last one."

"Is there anything I can do to help?"

"If you'll entertain little Babs for a while, I'll catch a catnap." Tess looked alarmed, and Lovey laughed. "I think I saw a rocking chair downstairs. You can't go wrong with a rocking chair, Tess."

"Come on, then, little one. Tell Mommy goodbye, and we'll go downstairs for a grand old rocking-chair adventure." Tess grinned at Lovey.

Mick was sprawled on the deck of a sailboat, covered only with a towel, and Tess was sitting nearby, combing her wet hair and singing. The song was one of his favorites, "Can't Help Lovin' Dat Man." Her beautiful voice lulled him, and he drifted near the edge of sleep, the boat rocking gently from side to side. The singing grew more distinct, and he came up out of the fringes of sleep to listen to the words.

Tess sang of being sad when her lover left and happy when he came back, and Mick knew she was singing to him. Opening his eyes, he lifted himself onto his elbow. He wasn't on a sailboat at all; he was in Johnny's house with Johnny's white sheets tangled around his naked body. But the song was real. Tess's voice drifted up the staircase, as clear as a summer day.

Mick slid into his shorts and jeans and hurried down the stairs, barefoot. When he reached the bottom step, he sat down. Tess was in the rocking chair, holding Lovey's baby and singing. It was a picture too beautiful to disturb.

Mick watched and listened and coveted. What if that were their baby Tess held? What if she were singing blues lullabies to a tiny baby girl with her red hair and his blue eyes? Mick knew what her name would be. Jenny. He and Tess had picked it out many years ago.

Grief gathered in his heart for what might have been, and he sat on the bottom step, watching Tess rock Lovey's baby, and mourned for Jenny.

"I wonder where you are, Jenny, my girl?" he said softly.

Was she up there with the angels, crying because he and Tess had never given her a chance to be born? Was she dreaming of strawberry ice-cream cones and pony rides and teddy bears and grand adventures with her daddy, carried high on his shoulders, giddy with excitement as he pointed out the different animals at the zoo or named the constellations or showed her the fireflies on a summer evening?

Mick rose from the stairs and walked softly across the room until he was standing behind the rocking chair. Tess slowed her rocking and glanced over her shoulder. Her eyes lit in the center, but she didn't stop singing. Leaning over the back of the chair, he noticed that the baby was almost asleep.

He tiptoed around the chair and sat on the sofa, facing them, one bare foot propped on his knee.

"I heard you singing," he said, quietly so as not to wake the baby.

"I'm baby-sitting for Lovey and Jim."

"You look natural, Tess."

"I don't feel natural. I'm a little scared of this tiny bundle."

He was somewhat in awe himself, but he didn't say so. Tess rocked and Mick watched, and finally he got up enough courage to say, "Do you think she'd mind if I held her awhile?"

"Let me ask her." Tess leaned close to the sleepy baby. "Little one, there's a big man sitting on the sofa who is dying to hold you. I think he's all right, but I wouldn't want to hand you over without getting your opinion."

Baby Babs yawned and blinked her blue eyes. Tess smiled up at Mick.

"I think she said yes."

Tess stood up, and they met in front of the rocking chair. They made the transfer from her arms to his as carefully as if they were negotiating world peace. After Mick had the baby, Tess kept her hand under Babs's bottom.

"She seems to be sagging, Mick."

"I'll fix that." He pulled the baby closer to his chest, and somehow Tess got tangled in with the baby and he ended up holding on to both of them.

He looked at her flushed face and grinned.

"This baby-sitting does have its compensations. I don't know who is the sweetest package, you or the baby."

"You're still full of Irish blarney, aren't you, Mick?"

"Only with you, Tess. You always seem to bring out my charm."

Laughing, Tess took a seat on the sofa and watched while Mick made the acquaintance of baby Babs, his head bent close and one hand cupping the tiny face.

"Sure and if you're not a wee angel come straight down from heaven to gladen the heart of your old uncle Mick." He glanced up at Tess. "I think she smiled at me."

"I have no doubt about it."

"Look at her tiny hands, Tess. See how she hangs on to me. I think she loves me."

"Hmmm," was all Tess could manage to say, for she had a huge lump in her throat.

"Did you see her little feet?" Mick kissed the sole of one tiny foot. "This baby is a miracle."

Tess wiped her tears with the sleeve of her robe, blinking away the feathers that tried to get into her eye. It was far too late to cry over what might have been.

Jim came down the stairs and reclaimed his baby.

"Feeding time for this little one."

Tess felt a dreadful sense of loss when Jim carried the baby back upstairs. She sat on the sofa, staring at Mick, slumped in his chair. She had never seen him slump. It seemed to her there was something she should say. But what would it be? *I'm sorry?* She was, of course, sorry for all the things they had missed—the babies with pink-soled feet, the midnight feedings, the birthday parties, the exhilarating feeling of being called Mommy and Daddy.

In the end she decided it was best to say nothing. After all, today they would be saying good-bye. Forever.

She stood up and quietly left the room. A single purple feather drifted to the floor behind her.

Mick sat in his chair until he could no longer hear her steps on the stairs; then he picked up the feather.

"Dear Tess . . . always leaving a trail." He turned it this way and that, and it seemed to him that he could see her reflection in the deep purple feather. "Is that so I can follow you wherever you go?"

He pressed his lips against the feather, then put it in his pocket. How could he follow Tess? They were going in different directions.

• • •

By ten o'clock that morning everyone except Lovey was downstairs. It was Sunday morning, and they were going to say a formal good-bye to Babs.

With Johnny in the lead, they trooped into the rose garden behind the house. The sun slanted across the roses, and distant church bells rang out their melodies of worship.

Johnny placed Babs on a stone bench in the center of the garden. Then, with his hands folded across his chest, he gave a simple eulogy. One by one, the friends came forward and said good-bye to Babs. Each one spoke from the heart.

And when the ceremony was over, Johnny gathered Babs and led the way to his station wagon. Lovey waved good-bye from the second-story bedroom window. They were silent on the drive to the airport where Mick's Cessna Skyhawk waited.

When they were all in the plane, Mick in the pilot's seat and Tess in the seat beside him, Johnny leaned over and plucked Tess's sleeve.

"I want you to be the one, Tess." She knew what he meant. They were going to scatter Babs's ashes over the Mississippi River.

"Are you sure, Johnny?"

"Yes. I know this is what she wants. We talked about it many times. She always said to me, 'Johnny, take me high into the sky and scatter me over the Mississippi. That way I can always be traveling to new places. Who knows how far the river will take me?' " He dashed a tear from his eye. "I can't do it, Tess. I'm too selfish to let her go."

Tess took the urn. "I'll do it, Johnny."

"Will you sing while you do it? She'd like that."

"Yes. I'll sing."

"Thank you, Tess." Satisfied, Johnny sat back

and strapped himself in. "Ready when you are, Mick."

Mick nodded. Just before he took the controls, he reached over and squeezed Tess's hand. She looked down at their joined hands for a second, then up at him. Their gazes touched, lingered, then pulled apart. Mick released her and took the Cessna into the sky.

Tess watched the way he handled the plane with such ease. He'd always been fascinated with flight. She remembered the day he'd got his license. They had cut classes, packed a picnic hamper, and rented a plane. He'd flown all the way to the Gulf Coast for a celebration. And what a celebration. She could still feel the sun on her face and the wind in her hair as they'd made love on a secluded sandy beach.

They flew in silence through crystal sky and shining cloud castles with the roar of the engine in their ears. Far below, the earth divided itself into patches of green and brown with an occasional gray ribbon threading across the landscape.

"River coming up," Mick shouted, pointing downward.

Tess nodded. Mick took the plane down, skimming the treetops. Tess still knew how to open the window. It was one of the many things Mick had taught her. When he dipped his right wing, she began to sing.

"Shall we gather at the river, where bright angel feet have trod . . ." Her voice rose sweet and clear above the sound of the engine, and she tipped the urn toward the Mississippi, still singing.

The sun caught Babs's ashes and turned them to gold; then the shimmering pieces separated and drifted downward into the waiting river.

"Soon we'll reach the shining river." Tess sang the familiar hymn. "Soon our pilgrimage will cease; soon our happy hearts will quiver with the melody of peace."

Mick climbed high into the sky, then turned the plane in a graceful curve and descended toward the river once more.

"Saints protect you, Babs," he said.

"Farewell, dear friend," Tess added.

"So long, my friend," Jim said. "We'll miss you."

"Be happy, my darling. Wherever you are, be happy," said Johnny, his face pressed against the window.

When they arrived back in Tupelo, Mick was the first to say good-bye. They were in Lovey's bedroom. Little Babs lay curled in a tiny ball in the middle of the bed, sleeping.

"I guess it's time to be moving on," Mick said, shaking hands with Jim and Johnny. He gave Lovey a bear hug, saving Tess for last.

She stood with her back to the window, facing all her friends. When Mick approached her, she didn't know what to expect, but he folded her in a bear hug, just as he had done with Lovey. She caught him close, absorbing his warmth and strength.

"Good-bye, Tess, my girl," he whispered, leaning close to her ear. "Be well."

"You, too, Mick."

He held her, then abruptly turned away. She couldn't bear to watch him go.

"Johnny, can I borrow the car?" she asked, already striding toward the door.

"Sure thing, Tess. The keys are on the hall table."

"Thanks." As she left the room, she heard the

voices of the three men mingling in a chorus of parting.

She ran down the stairway, jerking up the keys in her headlong flight to the car. By the time she got behind the wheel, she was panting, but not from exertion. There was nothing wrong with her physical condition; there was something wrong with her heart. It was bleeding and cracked and threatening to break.

She drove blindly away from Johnny's house, not knowing where she was going, not caring. She had to get away from Mick Flannigan. If she had stayed to watch him walk away with his bags, she might have screamed, or cried—or both. This time he would really disappear from her life. Before, it had seemed that he had taken an extended trip and could be expected to return at any moment. Even while she was married to Carson, then to O'Toole, she had the feeling they were merely filling in until Flannigan came back.

Funny, she had never known that until now, until she'd heard Mick say good-bye. Maybe she'd unconsciously been expecting him back because he hadn't said good-bye the first time.

Tess found herself on Joyner Street, near the park. On impulse she pulled in, parked the car, and made her way to the redwood bench where she and Flannigan had watched the fireflies. It was too early for them to be out, but still she could feel the evening approach. There was a languorous end-of-the-day feeling in the air. It was almost hypnotic.

She closed her eyes and let peace seep into her soul. Flannigan would probably be taking his bags down the staircase now. No, he wouldn't have suitcases. He would have a scruffy old duffel bag, probably the same one he'd had ten years ago.

Johnny—and perhaps Jim—would take him to the airport.

She cocked her head, listening. It seemed that she could hear the roar of Mick's Cessna Skyhawk as it climbed into the sky. If she tilted her head, she figured she would see a tiny silver speck, disappearing over the horizon.

She felt tears gather behind her eyes, and she batted her eyelashes to hold them in.

"I won't cry. This time I won't cry."

"Whatever is wrong, 'tis not worth your tears." The voice sounded out of the darkness behind her.

Tess jumped, then turned to see who was talking to her. An old man stood beside an oak tree, staring at her from a face as brown and gnarled as the tree trunk. His white hair and beard were long and scraggly, as if he hadn't seen the inside of a barbershop for a long time; and he was dressed all in black. The black suit was at least two sizes too big, the pants bagging at the knees, and the jacket sleeves rolled up over his knobby wrists.

"Are you speaking to me?" Tess asked.

"That I am."

He came out of the shadows, and Tess got a closer look. His suit had a frayed satin collar and a distinctive satin stripe down the sides of the pants. A tuxedo.

She was astonished and curious and not at all afraid. In her career she'd dealt with all kinds of people, and she considered herself a pretty good judge of character. The old man had a lively walk and a perky smile, and his blue eyes were as friendly as a spaniel puppy's.

When he reached the redwood bench, he gave her a polite, formal bow.

"Would you mind very much if I sat beside you?"

"Not at all."

"My name's Casey." He held out his hand.

"I'm Tess Jones. Glad to meet you, Mr. Casey."

"Just Casey." He inched closer and stared at her with bright blue eyes. They reminded her of Flannigan, and she had to look away. "Are you new here, Tess? I haven't seen you in the park before."

"I grew up in Tupelo, but I've been gone a long time."

"So, what brings you home?"

"The death of a dear friend."

"A great sadness, the loss of friends. It hurts nearly as much as the loss of family." His eyes grew watery, and he wiped them with his handkerchief. "Such a sadness, the loss of family." He sniffed loudly, then honked his nose.

"Mr. Casey . . ."

"Just Casey, if you please." The old man smiled at her through his tears.

Tess melted like ice cream in the sun. Mick used to accuse her of having the world's most tender heart, and she guessed he was right.

"Is something wrong?" she asked, leaning forward.

"Oh, my dear . . ." He paused, gazing off into the distance. "No concern of yours." He sniffed again, shifting so he could see her out of the corner of his eye.

"Oh, please. I hate to see you cry. Please let me help you if I can."

Casey praised all the saints he knew and a few he didn't. Lady Luck was finally smiling on him. He guessed there might be a miracle for old Casey after all.

"Well . . ." Casey's tears dried miraculously. "I can't find my son. He's all I have, you know, all

I have in this world. I've been searching and searching . . . for years I've been searching."

"How did you . . . get lost from him?"

"You see, my beautiful wife died, God rest her soul. Back in those days 'twasn't easy for a man to take care of a baby and his job too. The welfare took him away from me."

"How awful."

"I did the best I could by him, but I had a hard time keeping help, you see."

"Where did they take him?"

"First one family and then the other. I kept up with him for a while, and then . . . I was out on the job, traveling, you know, selling shoes, and I got lost from him entirely. When I got home, they had sent him away, south, some said. I never found him again."

"That's heartbreaking." Tess thought of Flannigan. Until he ran away and joined the circus, he'd been in an orphanage in Pass Christian, on the Gulf Coast.

"I'm getting old now. My fondest dream is to see him one more time before I die."

"Is there someone who can help you? Some agency?"

"Alas, Tess, agency people don't care much about folks who need their help. They only seem to care about drawing government paychecks." Casey sighed. "No, I'm afraid that, like Blanche, I have to depend on the kindness of strangers." He gave her a sidelong glance.

Tess was nobody's fool. She knew Casey was playing on her heartstrings, but she didn't mind. This poor old man with his faded tuxedo and his elegant speech needed her. And right now, with Flannigan flying out of her life forever, she especially needed to be important to someone.

"Look," she said, turning to Casey, "I have a few more days before I have to be back in Chicago. Tell me more about your son, and perhaps I can help you."

"Well . . ." Casey closed his eyes, as if he were remembering. "He had the blackest hair you ever saw, curly, too, just like his mother's. And he had the clearest blue eyes in the world. Pure Irish just like me and his mom." Casey paused, dabbing his damp face with his handkerchief.

Tess held her breath, knowing she was jumping to quite unwarranted conclusions, but wanting to believe anyway. Casey could have been describing Flannigan.

"He'd be about your age, I'd guess," Casey continued, "early thirties. Memory fails me sometimes."

Tess stared into his eyes. Blue. So blue. Just like Mick's. Wouldn't it be remarkable if she had somehow stumbled onto Flannigan's father? It could all fit. Mick had never been certain how he came to be in the orphanage.

"I imagine he'd be a strapping, big man." He looked down at his own small frame. "His mother was a big, handsome woman."

Tess jumped off the bench. Flannigan would be leaving town soon. In fact, he might be gone already.

"If you'll come with me, I think I can help you." She started running toward the car, then looked back to see old Casey puffing to keep up. She went back and took his hand. "Hurry. Please hurry."

After she had buckled him into Babs's sports car, she roared through the streets, taking the curves practically on two wheels.

"There's really no urgency about this, my dear," Casey said mildly, hanging on to the dashboard.

"Yes, there is. He might already be gone."

"Who?"

"Flannigan."

Casey smiled and clutched the armrest as Tess came to a tire-blistering stop in front of an elegant antebellum home.

"Wait here," she said, then she was out of the car and running up the steps. "Mick. Mick!"

A slim man with graying hair came to the front door. "Tess, is anything wrong?"

"I have to see Mick. Is he still here, Johnny?"

"He has already gone, Tess. We left him at the airport not ten minutes ago."

"Oh, God . . ."

She ran back toward the car, and Johnny called after her. "Tess?"

"I'll explain later," she called over her shoulder. Then she slid behind the wheel and roared off in another direction.

Flannigan's plane sat on the tarmac, waiting for him. He usually approached the plane with a sense of exhilaration, for he loved flying, loved being high above the rest of the world, far removed from reality, going someplace wonderful and adventurous because it was someplace new.

Today his footsteps dragged, and his duffel bag felt fifty pounds heavier. He didn't want to leave. And he knew why—Tess.

He tossed his bag into his plane and climbed into the pilot's seat. But he didn't gear up for flight. Instead he sat there, staring out over the runway.

Suddenly Tess was in his field of vision, her skirt and her red hair both whipping around her face. She was calling his name as she ran.

He jumped down from the plane.

"Tess? Tess!" He raced toward her, and they met at the edge of the tarmac. He caught her shoulders, and she reached for his face. They stood that way for a while, gazing at each other, speechless. Her hands moved softly over his cheeks, and he knew the feeling of almost-heaven.

When the wonder of seeing her again had diminished, he pulled her into the lee of the terminal.

"How did you get out here, past all the security?"

"I used my winning ways."

He laughed. "There are a few people inside who will never be the same."

"Mick. Oh, Mick." Her hands moved over his face once more. "I'm so glad I've found you."

"I am, too, love." He cupped her head, tangling his fingers in her silky hair. "We didn't say good-bye properly."

"We never do."

"It's time to remedy that."

He bent down, his lips almost touching hers, his eyes shining brighter than all the stars of heaven. She wanted to merge with him, body to body, heart to heart, and let the rest of the world go by. She wanted to stop time and join herself to him in a kiss that would last forever.

She moved closer. His heart thudded against her chest, and his breath was warm on her cheek.

"Mick," she said, scarcely louder than a sigh.

"Tess, my girl . . ."

"I didn't come to say good-bye."

His head jerked up, and prickles of fear marched along his skin.

"Is something wrong, Tess? Has something happened to Lovey and the baby?"

"Oh, no. It's nothing like that. I'm sorry I frightened you." She stepped back, her face shining with pleasure. "This is good news, Mick. Now, I don't want you to get your hopes up or anything like that. I could be wrong."

"You always did know how to make a man wait till Christmas. Out with it, my girl."

"I think I've found your father."

Six

"My father?" Mick gripped her shoulders. "What are you saying, Tess?"

"I met an old man in City Park, and he told me how he'd been looking for his son for years." She caught his arms. "Mick, he described *you*."

"Ahh, Tess. Tess, my girl." Mick lifted one of her hands to his lips and kissed it. "There must be a thousand men who look like me."

"Never. Not a single one. You're special, Mick Flannigan."

"You could be a bit prejudiced," he said, but he was pleased all the same. He hadn't felt special in years, not since he'd left Tess, as a matter of fact. "Tess, my darling, you've probably come across a lonely old man who touched that tender heart of yours. You were always picking up scraggly, broken-down creatures."

"Casey's a bit scraggly, but he's not broken-down. In fact, he'd be quite elegant if his clothes fit."

"Casey?"

"That's his name. Irish, like yours. And his

eyes . . ." Her own eyes glowed as she talked. "You should see them, Mick. Exactly like yours. As blue as the bonny blue sky."

Mick got caught up in her dream. His father. He could picture him, tall and elegant, his dark hair graying at the temples, his speech rich with Irish cadences.

"I'll just take a look at this man, Tess. Where is he?"

"In the car." She grabbed his hand and fairly tugged him back through the terminal and out the front door where the car waited with Casey inside. "There he is, Mick."

Mick saw the snow-white hair and beard, the weathered old face. For a moment he expected the heavens to open and choirs of angles to sing. He expected a ghostly hand to write across the sky, *Mick Flannigan, this is your father.*

But the dream lasted only a moment. He didn't believe in impossible dreams anymore.

The old man turned his head as Mick opened the door. Their eyes met. Casey was a con artist. Mick knew it immediately. Uncle Arthur had been the consummate con artist. It would have been impossible for Mick not to recognize one when he saw him.

"My name is Mick Flannigan."

He held out his hand. The old man took it in a surprisingly firm grip for one who looked so frail.

"I'm Casey." Casey stepped from the car, moving as elegantly as if he were stepping from the podium in front of a symphony orchestra. His tuxedo sagged around him as he faced Mick.

"Tess thinks you might be my father," Mick said, giving him a straight look that said, *I know your kind.*

"Well, now." Casey tilted his head this way and

that, like a cocky old mockingbird. He cast a sidelong glance at Tess, then slid his gaze back to Mick. Finally he took a step backward. "Alas. You are not my son."

"How do you know I'm not? I understand you haven't seen your son in years."

Tears sprang to Casey's eyes, and Mick was impressed. *Damn the old con artist.* Mick had always admired a good one, and Casey was good.

"A father would recognize his own son." Casey placed his hand over his baggy suit somewhere in the vicinity of his heart. "I would know in here."

"Oh," said Tess, disappointment clearly written in her face. "Mick, what are we going to do?"

Mick decided that fate was either a trickster or a genius. His plane was still on the tarmac, and Tess was looking at him with tears in her eyes. He didn't believe in spitting in the face of fate.

"Tess, my darling, what we're going to do is help Casey."

"Do you mean that, Mick? You'll help?"

"Now, Tess. When have you known me to turn a stranger from my door? Of course I'll help."

He thought Casey looked a mite relieved. As well he should. Mick would have a talk with him later, a very long, very private talk.

But for now, his main concern was protecting Tess. He didn't know how she had managed all those years without him. How could he have forgotten her penchant for dragging home strays? When they'd been at Mississippi State, she'd always been rescuing lame dogs and starving cats. Rescuing a human being was a different matter. There could be a certain element of danger in getting tangled up in the affairs of another human being.

He'd watch over her, though. He wasn't going

anywhere in particular, so a few more days wouldn't matter. He'd get this business with Casey settled. Then he'd say good-bye to Tess. Really say good-bye.

Mick draped his arm around Tess's shoulders. She had such slim, elegant shoulders. Fragile-feeling. He'd never noticed that about her before.

"Why don't we gather Mr. Casey's things—"

"Just Casey," the old man interrupted.

"Okay. Then we'll go back to Johnny's house and make plans."

Mick climbed behind the wheel of the car, and Casey directed them back to City Park.

"You left your things there?" Tess asked as they followed Casey back toward the redwood bench.

"No. I live there."

"You *live* there?" Tess looked at Mick, but he didn't say anything. He didn't even seem surprised.

"It's not so bad, really." Casey led them into the woods until they came upon a large cardboard box. Several black garbage bags covered the outside of the box, but some of the lettering showed through. It was a refrigerator box. "Of course, when it rains, my house gets soggy, then I have to go out and find a new one."

He disappeared into the box. Tess and Flannigan could hear him inside, singing softly to himself.

"In the sweet by and by. We will meet on that beautiful shore. In the sweet by and byy . . ."

"Tess." Mick tipped up her face. "I don't want you to get your hopes up about this old man."

"I only want to help him."

"We will. We'll do what we can."

"Thank you for staying, Mick."

"I don't have an adoring public waiting for me where I'm going, Tess."

"Where are you going?"

"I was thinking of Texas. Remember how we used to talk about Texas?"

"You were going to fly, and I was going to wait for you in a field of bluebonnets, singing to our babies." Tess's eyes were misty.

"It was a good dream once."

"It still would be . . . if we were in love."

"Yes . . . if we were in love."

During the course of their conversation they had stepped back some distance from the box, and Mick had unconsciously moved so close to Tess, they were joined shoulder to shoulder and hip to hip. He separated himself from her.

"I think what we should do," he said, "is find a place to sleep tonight, and then bright and early tomorrow morning take Casey to the Welfare Department so those people can take care of him."

"You said you'd help." Tess looked at him with accusing eyes.

"I'm going to." He waved his hand toward the refrigerator box. "Look at that, Tess. He lives in a cardboard box. He wears threadbare clothes. The Welfare Department will feed and clothe him and find him decent housing."

"What about his son?"

"How do you know he even has a son?"

"When did you get to be so cynical, Mick Flannigan? He *told* me so."

"Tess . . ."

Flannigan reached for her, but she flung herself away from him, waving her arms dramatically.

"Just go on and leave us alone. We don't need your help. I'll find Casey's son all by myself."

"Dammit, Tess. You're being stubborn."

"You're being heartless."

"Wanting to give the old man clothes and food and a place to live is not heartless."

What he should do, he thought, was get into his Skyhawk and fly off and never look back. Tess Jones was nothing but a passel of trouble. She was hard to handle besides.

They glared at each other in the waning light of day. Inside the refrigerator box, the singing had stopped.

"Look, Tess. I only stayed to keep you out of trouble—"

"Keep me out of trouble!" She jutted out her chin and glared at him. Everything about her sparked with anger, her eyes, her hair, her body. "The only trouble I ever had was with you."

His hot blood roared in his ears, and he turned his back to her and stalked off.

"Good. Leave!" she yelled. "You always did leave when the going got tough!"

"Hell." He stalked back to her, then caught her and dragged her close, tipping up her chin with his hand. "Do you want me to help look for a man who probably doesn't exist?"

"No. *You* go to Texas or Timbuktu or wherever your wandering feet take you, and *I'll* look for Casey's son."

"Tess . . ." He could never stay mad at her, especially when he was touching her. "Ahhh, Tess, my girl." He folded her next to his heart and pressed his face into her fragrant hair. "For you, I'll chase Casey's rainbow."

With her face against his shoulder she smiled. "I knew you would all along. You're nothing but a big old soft-hearted teddy bear."

"Humph," he muttered, but he was pleased all the same. He'd missed being somebody's teddy bear.

He released her, then stepped back and lit a cigar. It gave him something to do with his hands. Then he said, "I'll go with you on this wild-goose chase—but only for a little while . . . only until you can see the truth."

"We'll see." She smiled her satisfied Mona Lisa smile. It was the one she always smiled when she knew she'd won a battle with Flannigan.

He clamped his teeth down hard on his cigar. He'd never stopped loving her, that much was true. But at the moment he was very close to being smitten by her all over again. Being in love and knowing he had to be noble was one thing. But being smitten was something else entirely. Being smitten caused a man to do impulsive things, foolish things.

He blew smoke rings into the night and watched them disintegrate. The search for Casey's mythical son could possibly be the most dangerous journey of Flannigan's life.

Joy bubbled in his soul and spilled over. His laughter startled a rabbit nearby.

"What's so funny, Mick?"

"Remember the last trip we took together, Tess?"

"How could I forget? That old hearse broke down on the Pennsylvania Turnpike, and we ended up in one of those barns with a hex sign painted on the side."

"Remember the look on that old lady's face when she saw the hearse? She thought we had come to take her husband."

"'But he ain't dead yet,'" Tess said, imitating their long-ago hostess, "'he's just drunk.'"

She reached for his hand, and he took it. "That was a long time ago, Mick."

"Yes. A long time ago."

"Well, here I am." Casey emerged from his box.

He was carrying a small bundle tied with an old blue bandanna and a walking cane with a tarnished gold head. He smiled at both of them, showing two rows of very white teeth, a little too large for his mouth. "I feel like Dorothy setting off to the Land of Oz."

"I'm afraid there won't be any magic this trip, Casey." Mick took his bundle and his arm, and led him toward the car.

"You never know," Casey said.

They ended up that night in two rooms at a small motel outside Tupelo—Tess in one room and Casey and Flannigan in the other. Johnny had insisted they stay with him, but they hadn't wanted to impose. They had collected Tess's cat and her clothes; then Johnny had driven them to a car-rental agency. The sturdy Ford Mick had rented stood outside the door of unit four.

Lights glowed in the windows of units three and four, and then shortly after midnight the lights in unit four went out. Mick lay in the dark with his feet hanging off the end of the bed. Motel beds were always too short for him. He listened for sounds from the other room. Through the thin walls he heard the television click on. A short time later it clicked off. The plumbing between the walls rattled. Tess was showering.

He rolled himself in his sheet and shut his eyes. He didn't want to think about Tess with water beading her skin.

Now she was singing. He raised himself on his elbow, listening. The words sounded true and clear through the partition that separated them. Tess was singing the hauntingly beautiful love song from *Carousel*, "If I Loved You."

Tears squeezed under his eyelids, and he was not ashamed. One of the good things Uncle Arthur had taught him was that it was okay for boys to cry. Men too.

"Think of me my darling," he said. Then he lay back on his pillow and drifted asleep, lulled by the sound of Tess's voice.

Tess huddled under her covers, gravitating naturally toward the warmest spot in the bed. The spot was not only warm, it was also big and bulky and solid. She hugged her arms around it and snuggled close, blissful, even in her sleep.

The warm spot moved, and she followed it, hooking her legs around it this time so it would remain steady. When it moved again, she came out of her slumber.

She sat up in bed, one strap of her nightgown sliding down her shoulder. When her eyes adjusted to the dark, she saw why her warm spot had kept moving.

"Mick Flannigan, what are you doing in my bed?"

"Lie back down and go to sleep, Tess."

He rolled over, taking half the covers with him, and presented her with his broad, naked back.

"And you without a stitch of clothes on, I'll bet." She ran her hands under the covers to check out her theory.

"It's best to let sleeping dogs lie," he grunted, moving out of her reach. He yawned hugely, stretching his arms over his head. Then he crossed them on his chest and shut his eyes.

"You look like something freshly laid out in a casket. Get up from there, Flannigan."

He sat up and propped himself against the headboard.

"Here I am, and here I'll stay. I'd planned on

getting a good night's sleep, but if you want to chatter, I'm awake now, and I'll listen for about two minutes."

"What are you doing in my room?"

"Casey snores."

"So do you. Since when has a little snoring bothered you?"

"Since it sounds like a freight train."

Tess flopped against the headboard beside him, pulling up the strap of her gown.

"I don't suppose I need even bother to ask how you got in."

"I'm the one who taught you to pick locks, remember?"

"It was one of the more useful things you taught me."

Now that she was wide awake and her eyes had adjusted to the dark, she glanced around her room. Mick's clothes lay in a heap on top of her sequined shoes. One toe was peeking out from under his jeans, winking at her.

The sight of their clothes tangled together made her nostalgic.

"Flannigan, what am I going to do with you?"

He swiveled his head so he could see her better. Her hair shone in the dark, and her gown was a soft rosy sheen that beckoned to him. Desire smote him so hard he had to clamp his jaws together to keep from groaning.

Silently he cursed the impulse that had driven him to her bed. What in the hell was he doing? Sure, Casey had been snoring. But that wasn't the reason he had slipped through the darkness and picked Tess's lock and climbed in beside her sleek, warm body.

The reason was insanity. Plain and simple. Tess Jones was driving him insane. It had started when

LET YOURSELF BE LOVESWEPT BY... SIX BRAND NEW LOVESWEPT ROMANCES!

Because Loveswept romances sell themselves ...we want to send you six (Yes, six!) exciting new novels to enjoy for 15 days — risk free! — without obligation to buy

Discover how these compelling stories of contemporary romances tug at your heart strings and keep you turning the pages. Meet true-to-life characters you'll fall in love with as their romances blossom. Experience their challenges and triumphs — their laughter, tears and passion.

Let yourself be Loveswept! Join our **at-home reader service!** Each month we'll send you six new Loveswept novels **before they appear in the bookstores.** Take up to **15 days to preview** current selections **risk-free! Keep only those shipments you want.** Each book is yours for only $2.25 plus postage & handling, and sales tax in N.Y. — **a savings of 50¢ per book** off the cover price.

NO OBLIGATION TO BUY — WITH THIS RISK-FREE OFFER!

YOU GET SIX ROMANCES RISK FREE...
Plus AN EXCLUSIVE TITLE FREE!

Loveswept Romances

she'd sauntered up the walk at Johnny's house, and every day it had got worse. Every song she sang drove him closer to the edge. Every time she laughed, he felt pieces of himself flying off and landing at her feet. Every time she touched him, a big chunk of his heart broke off and became hers forever. Now, he was broken into a million pieces, and only Tess could put him back together again.

Honor and nobility be damned. He was in her bed because he wanted her. Selfish, that's what he was. The question was not what she was going to do, but what *he* was going to do.

"What you're going to do, Tess, my girl, is lie back down on that side of the bed and get a good night's sleep." He reached for her with the intention of tucking her in. His plan was to be matter-of-fact and nonchalant so she wouldn't see how much he wanted her. He was also going to stuff plenty of covers between them so he wouldn't be tempted to change his mind.

When he touched her, she trembled. Tucking her in wasn't going to be as easy as he'd thought.

"We used to kiss, Flannigan," she whispered, her eyes huge and shining. "We used to kiss until one of us got sleepy."

"I remember." God, he remembered only too well. He scooted closer so he could handle her better— tucking her in—and she smiled at him. He felt as if a jagged blade had pierced his heart. "If we got started now, we might not stop."

"Speak for yourself, Flannigan." She reached up and curled her hands in his hair. "I can stop with you anytime I want to."

He called on all the saints he knew to protect him from his own folly. He should never have come to her bed.

"That's good, Tess. You've learned some restraint in your old age."

"Restraint!" She lunged at him. He caught her, and they both tumbled back to the mattress. She battered at his chest, her eyes blazing as brightly as her hair. "You let go of me, Mick Flannigan. I don't need you to tell me how to behave." Tears sprang to her eyes. "I've never needed you. Never!" She bucked under him.

He was astonished. And alarmed. He sat up and straddled her, pinning her to the bed. Her fists kept flailing his chest. He ignored them.

"Easy girl. Calm down."

"I don't want to calm down." Her fists battered at him. "All my life people have been trying to remake me. Don't you start with me, Flannigan."

He caught her flying fists, then rolled over, wrapping her tightly in his arms.

"Who has tried to remake you, my darling?" She struggled against him. "Who?"

"Everybody." Her voice was muffled against his chest. "Nobody," she said, stronger this time. "Let me go, Flannigan."

"Ahhh, Tess." He began to stroke her hair. "Tess, my love." Strands of her hair clung to his hands, curled possessively around his fingers. "You've always been perfect in my eyes. Always."

"Do you mean it, Flannigan?"

"I mean it." His hands moved lower, stroking her back.

"Then why did you leave?"

"It had nothing to do with you." She grew stiff and silent. Even his caresses couldn't rouse her to life again. "My Lord. What have I done to you?"

He eased away from her so he could see her face. She looked like a china doll, beautiful and perfect and lifeless.

"Tess, my love, my darling."

His mouth covered hers. She remained stiff and unyielding. He wrapped her close, molding her against his body, rocking back and forth on the bed as he continued to kiss her.

"My love, my sweet." He felt the first flutter of response, and his heart soared. He leaned back again to see her face. Color was flowing into her skin again. "Saints be praised," he whispered as his mouth claimed hers once more.

She curled her hands in his hair. "Flannigan . . . Flannigan."

They spiraled backward in time. She was his and he was hers, and she was calling his name, over and over. He slid his hands down the back of her gown, and she arched against him. The thin layer of silk between them seemed to disintegrate.

His hands began to move, down her back and around her hips and over her legs.

"Mmmm," she said, closing her eyes and purring like a kitten under his touch.

"Do you still like that, Tess?"

"I never stopped liking it."

He slid his hand up her thigh. "Your legs are beautiful." His hand inched higher. "Silky." And higher. "Warm."

"Flannigan . . . Flannigan."

With his hand resting high on her thigh, he kissed her arm, her shoulder, her ear. Her skin felt just the way he remembered, cool and fragrant, with the pulse in her neck fluttering like fragile butterfly wings.

"You are mine," he murmured. "Always were, always will be."

He nudged aside her straps and moved his lips over her breasts, reclaiming what was his. "Here," he murmured, "and here . . . and here. It's all mine . . . all mine." Reckless with greed and hunger, he staked his claim all over her body. She grew wild under him, hot and wild, writhing at his touch, urging him on with her voice of music.

He tore her gown aside. The silk whispered in the darkness as it ripped, and then it lay on either side of her body, and she was offered up to him like an exotic flower. He explored her soft curves, delved into her warm hollows, and drank deeply of her sweetness.

She clung to him, singing his name. The music penetrated his heart, seeped into his soul.

"Tess, my love, my darling. Do you want me?"

"Flannigan, oh yes. Yes. Yes."

He came home then, slid into the deep, silky recesses of her body and found his way home. She wrapped her arms tightly around him, and they rejoiced together, moving in perfect harmony, dancing in perfect rhythm. At last, at long, long last, they both knew heaven.

They soared together, up among the stars with a heavenly chorus ringing in their ears. But the chorus was not angels: It was the combined voices of Tess and Flannigan, giving vent to the music of their hearts.

"I've dreamed of you like this." He eased to a slow, languorous rhythm, gazing down at her face. "Do you know how many times I've dreamed of this?"

"Two?" Her hips danced with his, and she smiled with sheer joy.

His laughter rang out richly in the darkness.

"I lied to you, my love. It took me more than two days to get over you."

Her fingernails dug into his back, and her face became fierce.

"Are you over me, Flannigan?" For a moment

they were still, straining toward each other, pulsing with tension. "Are you?" she whispered.

Her question pierced his heart and seared his soul. Looking down at her, with her hair spread across the pillows like flame and her eyes shining up at him with glory, he knew he could not lie. Not now.

"Never. I'll never be over you." He caught her fiercely to him, pressing his face in her hair and inhaling her fragrance.

They stayed that way, their bodies joined, their hearts thundering against each other.

"Never," he whispered once more as he began to move inside her. "Never." His voice and his movements became fierce. And suddenly they were caught up in a wild roller-coaster ride, thundering over the tracks, dipping and swaying and tilting. The exhilaration of the ride rose high in their throats, until they were both crying out their pleasure.

They careened over the tracks, going the same place and arriving at the same time. The ride came to a thundering, crashing stop.

"Ahh, Tess, my girl."

He pressed his face to her bosom, his arms circled around her. Then he tipped them over so they lay, facing each other, across the bed. "On stormy nights I used to lie in my bed—wherever I happened to be—and listen to wind blow and thunder crash and dream I held you in my arms. Remember how thunderstorms used to bring out the primitive in us, Tess?"

"We didn't need a thunderstorm tonight, did we?" She played with the curls that dipped across his forehead.

"We created our own." He traced her face with his fingertips. "I could kill them, you know."

"Who?"

"Your other husbands."

"Why?"

"Because I've always considered you mine." He hugged her close. "Always."

"Even after you left me?"

"Yes. Even then."

She pressed her forehead into the crook of his shoulder, underneath his chin. They stayed that way for a long, long time. Mick started stroking her back, the way he did so long ago, and she sighed.

"Mick . . ."

"Hmmm?"

"How long can you stay with us, with Casey and me?"

They shifted a little, and she turned her face so her cheek was pressed against his chest.

"As long as you need me, Tess. I don't have anyplace special to go, and I certainly don't have an important career waiting for me."

She thought of herself, back in the club in Chicago, standing on the stage all alone, singing blues songs and meaning them, then going home to an empty bed and a cat.

"My career isn't all that important."

He pulled his head back so he could see her face. In the dark it was a pale, beautiful outline.

"How can you say that? It's something you've worked for all your life. It's something you've always wanted."

"It's not all I've wanted, Mick." His eyes were so brilliant, so probing, she had to turn away. She feigned a huge yawn. "I don't know about you, but I'm getting sleepy."

"Tess . . ." Mick caught her chin. "Don't turn

away from me." He tugged her face around and they stared at each other for a long time.

What they had done dawned suddenly and simultaneously on them. He had reclaimed her, and she had let him. He called himself insane, and she called herself foolish.

It was too late to undo what had been done, but it was not too late to change the way things *would* be.

"You turned away first, Mick," Tess whispered.

A boulder settled on Mick's heart, and he let her go.

"So I did, Tess." He put his arms around her and positioned them correctly on the bed, their heads at the headboard and their feet pointing south. They lay side by side, staring straight ahead into the darkness.

"Good night, Tess."

"Good night, Mick."

Mick woke up with such a sense of peace that for a moment he thought he was back in college. In those days with Tess at his side, loving him, he'd been invincible. Or so he had thought.

Strange he should wake up feeling invincible again.

He rolled over in his bed, and there she was— Tess, by his side once more. Seeing her in his bed filled him with such a sense of well-being, he laughed out loud.

She didn't even stir. He tenderly brushed a strand of hair off her face, letting his hand linger on her soft cheek.

"Good morning, my love. Did you sleep well?"

The soft rise and fall of her breathing was his only answer.

"Did you dream of me?" He traced the sensuous curve of her lips with his index finger. "Did you lie on your side of the bed and wish you were on mine?" She burrowed into her pillow, still fast asleep. "I did. I lay in the dark for two hours trying to justify moving to your side of the bed and knowing what heaven felt like once more."

He leaned down and kissed her cheek; then he climbed out of bed. Last night had happened. He hadn't meant it to, but it had anyhow. And now it was over and done with. The best thing to do was go on as if nothing had changed—and make damned sure it didn't happen again.

"Ahhh, I'm such a noble man. Uncle Arthur would be disappointed if he could see me now."

He reached for his jeans, disturbing the cat who had made them into a comfortable nest for himself. O'Toole arched his back and spit. Then, seeing it was only Flannigan, he leaped onto the bed and assumed his Buddha position beside his mistress.

"Lucky cat. You have a right to be there and I don't."

O'Toole gave him a wise Siamese smile, then leaned down and licked Tess's shoulder. She moved. With another smile he licked her shoulder again.

"O'Toole?" Tess yawned and stretched, her eyes still closed. "Is that you?"

O'Toole purred. Tess came slowly out of her sleep, opening first one eye, and then the other. What she usually saw when she woke up was her cat. This morning the first thing she saw was Flannigan, standing in his shorts holding his jeans in one hand and her sequined shoes in the other.

"Well, good morning." She smiled. And then because she felt so good, she laughed.

Mick thought it was the most beautiful sound he'd ever heard. He imagined what it would be like to wake up to her laughter every morning for the rest of his life.

"Top of the day to you." He stuck one leg into his pants, never taking his eyes off her. "If I had known that was how to do it, I'd have done it myself."

"Do what?"

"Wake you up. The cat licks your shoulder to wake you up."

"I liked your way better, Flannigan."

He stood with one pants leg on and one off, watching her. She merely smiled, arching her back and stretching like a great big, satisfied cat herself.

"Don't play games with me, Tess."

"I'm not playing games. I'm merely saying I liked your way better."

His belt buckle thudded softly on carpet as he let go of his pants. Kicking them aside, he stalked to the bed. He leaned over her, forcing her backward against the pillows. Then he put one hand on either side of her, pinning her to the mattress.

"Close your eyes, Tess," he said softly.

"Why?"

"So I can wake you up my way."

Their eyes locked and held in mortal combat as they both struggled with passions that had never died and love that was fighting to be reborn.

"You wouldn't," she said finally.

"Wouldn't I?"

"You're too honorable."

"An honorable man always gives a lady what she wants."

A bead of sweat trickled from under her heavy hair and inched down the side of her face. Her entire body heated up, and she felt the sheet stick to her in damp patches.

Flannigan's eyes roamed up and down her body, and everywhere his gaze touched, she grew hotter. She was playing with fire, and she knew it. But she didn't care. She had survived being in his bed last night, and she was feeling bold and reckless. She wasn't thinking about getting hurt again— only about how far she could go with him and still come out a winner. It was a game she was playing. A dangerous game. And she was breaking all the rules.

"I quite agree, Flannigan." She smiled up at him from the pillows. "A man always gives a lady what she wants."

"Then, tell me, Tess." He leaned closer, so close his lips were almost touching hers. "What is it you want?"

"It's awfully early in the morning for such a hard question. What time is it, Flannigan?"

"Time for the truth." His lips brushed lightly against hers. "What do you want from me?"

"Hmmm, let me see." *Unconditional love*, her mind was screaming. "What I want from you is two pieces of toast, lots of butter—real, not the artificial kind—and one egg, scrambled, and a bowl of whole-wheat cereal with strawberries on the top, and a very large, very cold orange juice. And I'd like it on a silver tray with a red rose."

"You always did have the appetite of a stevedore . . . for all things."

"You asked what I wanted, Flannigan. Now, are you going to satisfy me?"

Laughing, he lifted her off the bed and tossed her over his shoulder.

"What are you doing?" She tried to wiggle off, but he held her still with one hand across her bottom and one hand on her legs.

"Tess, my girl, I'm going to give you everything you want."

Seven

He carried her into the bathroom and stepped into the shower.

"Flannigan, are you crazy?"

"With you, I am." He let her slide down his body, and when she was on her feet, he tipped up her chin and smiled at her. "You always did want a shower before breakfast. Especially after a night like last night."

He turned on the water, then shifted her around, reached for the soap, and began to lather her back. She shivered with pleasure.

"A little to the left, Flannigan. You missed a spot."

He smiled at a spot high on the shower wall. She was as high-spirited as an Irish filly. He began to hum a tune. She joined in, and soon they were harmonizing, singing snatches of the words, getting them wrong, laughing, and going on with the song anyhow.

When the shower was over, he wrapped her in a huge towel, carried her back to the bed, and propped her up against the headboard.

"Don't move from that spot." He dressed quickly and started toward the door.

"Where are you going?"

With his hand on the doorknob, he turned and grinned.

"Are you going to miss me while I'm gone?"

"Of course not." She tossed her damp hair back from her face. "I never miss the men who come and go in my life, Flannigan. I merely replace them."

"You'll have to move fast this time, for I'll be back soon."

He slipped through the door and eased it shut behind him. Tess sat on the bed staring at the door for a long time.

"O'Toole, what in the world am I going to do about Flannigan?"

She stretched on the bed. His pillow was still dented where he had laid his head. She drew the pillow into her arms and hugged it close.

"You'll leave me again, won't you?" She pressed her cheek against his pillow. "Just like the last time. Do you love me, Flannigan?"

Not enough to stay, she thought. Last night had changed nothing.

"Damn you, Mick Flannigan." She flung the pillow across the room. "You won't get to me this time." She hugged her arms around herself, and suddenly they weren't her arms: They were his. Her body quickened, ripened. She longed for him. She wanted him there by her side, in her arms, at any cost.

"Damn you." She rose from the bed, magnificent in her rage, and the towel slipped to the floor unnoticed. "I can spend every minute of every day making love with you, and still you can walk away and I won't care. I won't."

She stalked across the room and jerked her

clothes out of a suitcase. O'Toole, sensing a storm, gave her a wide berth.

"You're just another man." Her hands trembled as she slipped into her blouse. A tear splashed her cheek as she reached for her buttons. "You're just another ordinary man, Mick Flannigan."

Flannigan was whistling when he opened the door to his motel unit. Casey sat in the room's only chair, dressed in his baggy tuxedo, his beard and hair slicked down with water.

"Did you get up early or are you coming in late?" Casey asked.

"Are you going to be a nosy old man?" Mick came into the room, smiling, ripping his T-shirt over his head.

"Maybe I worry. Good to have somebody to worry about."

"Don't get too attached. We'll be finding your *real* son soon." He pulled a clean T-shirt on, and turned to give Casey a frank stare. "Isn't that right, Casey?"

Casey shifted in his chair, then lifted his chin and stared back at Mick, blue eyes boring into blue eyes.

"That's right. Pretty soon I'll have me a real family. A son of my very own. Who knows? Maybe even a beautiful little daughter-in-law. Babies too." As he warmed to his subject, his eyes began to twinkle. "I'm going to have lots of grandbabies, the fat, happy kind I can dandle on my knee."

Mick ran his hands through his hair and sat on the edge of the dresser, watching the old man.

"Who are you, Casey?"

"Yesterday I was a lonely old man living in a cardboard box."

"Before that."

"I'm southern aristocracy, educated at Yale, then Juilliard. I've conducted some of the finest symphonies in the world."

"How did you get from the podium to a box in the park?"

"It was a long and hard journey, via the bottle, but I'm clean and sober now."

"And your family . . . "

"Dead. Every one of them. I'm the only one left."

He was telling the truth. Mick could tell by the straightforward look in his eyes.

"I'm sorry, Casey."

"My own doing. I took a few wrong turns along the way."

Casey twirled his cane round and round, while Mick stared at the spinning gold top.

"Just so we understand each other, Casey. . . . I'm sticking around to see that Tess doesn't get hurt. I don't want you taking a wrong turn at her expense."

"Didn't you hurt her once?"

"What do you know?"

"Maybe I'm just guessing."

It was too much on target to be just a guess, but Mick decided to let it pass. For now.

"Just remember, I'll be watching you."

"I'll be watching you too, Flannigan."

They faced each other down, and then they both began to chuckle.

"You're a sly old bird," Flannigan said.

"Wait till you see me fly."

"You're going to get your chance—starting now. Can you drive."

"Yes."

"Good." Flannigan pulled a wad of bills out of his billfold and handed them to Casey. "Go to that fancy restaurant down the street and get two pieces of toast with real butter, one egg, scrambled, whole-wheat cereal with real cream and strawberries, and a large glass of orange juice. Bring it back on a silver platter. I don't care how you get it, short of stealing. Bribe, beg, do whatever is necessary, but it has to be on a silver platter. Do you understand?"

"Perfectly." Casey stood up, looking regal in spite of his baggy evening clothes. "You're going courting."

"No. I'm just giving a lady what she wants."

" 'Tis a certain lady with red hair, I'm thinkin', so I'll pick up a couple of steaks for you and me. Unless I miss my guess, we'll need all the strength we can get to handle her."

"Do that, Casey." Mick left the room, laughing.

Tess had requested a red rose, and he knew just where to get it. No hothouse flowers for him. No, sir. Tess would have the best. Nature's own.

He walked around to the back of the motel and climbed over the chain-link fence. Then he jumped the small ditch that separated the commercial property from a ritzy residential section. Through the green belt of trees he could see exactly the house he had in mind. It was a huge white colonial affair, complete with a gazebo and a rose garden.

Putting on his best smile, he skirted around the back of the house until he came to the street. Then he sauntered casually down the sidewalk as if he'd just stepped from a Rolls-Royce Silver Cloud.

He went up the steps and rang the doorbell. A wizened old woman with gray hair and a white apron came to the door.

"Excuse me, ma'am." Flannigan bowed and smiled. Then he whipped a white card out of his pocket and waved it in front of the old lady's nose.

"I'm Trent Cadburry from the Horticulture Society of the South, and I'm here to check your roses."

"Them ain't my roses. They belong to Miz Shumaker. I'm Lilla."

"May I speak with Mrs. Shumaker?"

"She ain't home."

"Oh dear." Flannigan flapped around, imitating a man in great distress.

"Is they somethin' I can do for you? You don't look too good."

"It's about the roses, you see, Miss Lilla. There's a dreadful disease going around, and it's my duty to take samples back to the lab for testing. If I don't get some of Mrs. Shumaker's roses, there's no telling how far this disease will spread."

"Shoot. Is that all you want? Some of them old roses? Why didn't you say so in the first place instead of all that carryin' on about Horseculture Society? Humph. I ain't studyin' no societies." Wiping her hands on her apron, she stepped onto the front porch.

Flannigan could hardly believe his good fortune. He had imagined his con would be worth about half a dozen roses. He'd even been willing to pay a fancy price. By the time Lilla got through beheading rosebushes, he was going to have to get a delivery truck to haul them in.

"Thank you, Miss Lilla. I can't tell you how much I appreciate this."

"Jest shut up and let me finish here. I'm tired of these old roses. Be glad to be shed of 'em."

When Lilla finally stood up, Flannigan's arms were loaded with roses of every color.

"This should do nicely, Miss Lilla. You don't know how much I appreciate your help."

"If you find out they's disease in 'em, don't come back here tellin' Miz Shumaker. Jest keep it to yourself. Maybe they'll all die." She dusted her hands together, then looked with satisfaction on the path of devastation she had left among the rosebushes.

The roses in Mick's arms fell naturally in all directions—some long-stemmed and some short—rose and pink and red and yellow and white and peach. A single black flower, taller than the rest, stood majestically in the center.

Flannigan thanked Lilla again, and left. Casey was waiting for him inside their room, holding a silver tray.

"Did you have any trouble?" Flannigan asked, scanning the tray to see if all the food was there.

"None. Did you?" Casey eyed the roses.

"Slick as clockwork." He put the roses in a big jar that had held artificial flowers. He added water and put the jar on the silver tray, then stood back to admire their handiwork.

"We make quite a team, Flannigan."

"Don't be getting any ideas, Casey."

"I wouldn't dream of it," he said, but he had his fingers crossed behind his back when he said it.

Tess was combing her hair when she heard the knock on her door.

"Who is it?"

"Who do you want it to be?"

Flannigan. Smiling, she laid her hairbrush aside.

"Is that you, Casey?"

"I should eat all these strawberries myself."

"You brought food?"

She flung open the door, and there was Flannigan, holding a silver tray of food and the biggest bunch of roses she had ever seen.

"Roses." She pressed her face into the blossoms.

"I love roses," she said, smiling at him across the rainbow of flowers. "Where on earth did you get them?"

"A rose garden."

"Whose rose garden?" He merely smiled at her, not answering, and she laughed. "Did you steal these roses, Mick?"

"I conned these roses, using my considerable charm."

"You slept with somebody for roses?"

He backed her into the room and kicked the door shut behind them. Then he plopped the tray on a small table by the window and pulled her into his arms.

"Do you consider me charming in bed, Tess, my girl?"

"I don't have enough evidence yet to answer your question."

He eyed the bed. "We could remedy that."

"My food would get cold."

She eased out of his arms, and he let her go. She supposed she should be grateful he didn't put up any resistance. In spite of telling herself that she could make love with him every minute of every day and still not lose her heart, she wasn't ready to test her theory. At least not yet. Not until she had a chance to recover from their first encounter.

She sat down in front of the breakfast tray and nibbled a piece of toast. All the foods she had requested were there, even the real butter on the toast. She looked up at Flannigan, lounging casually against the dresser, watching her eat. *He's just an ordinary man*, she kept telling herself; but what ordinary man would steal roses for her and bring breakfast on a silver tray to a dingy motel room?

She wasn't going to think about all that now, for

the trip was just beginning; and if she started thinking Flannigan was special, she'd lose her head for sure. She might even lose her heart.

She plucked a strawberry off the silver tray.

"Want some, Mick?"

"Yes." He moved slowly across the room, as if he were floating toward her from a great distance. "You remember how I like to eat my strawberries, don't you?"

She nodded, never taking her eyes from his. When he was almost at her side, she caught the strawberry between her lips. He leaned down, bracing himself with one hand on her shoulder, and closed his mouth over one end of the strawberry. The sweet juice squished between their lips. They savored the berries, the juice, but most of all they savored the moment. Once again they had slipped back in time, back into a love ritual that came as naturally to them as if they had done it only yesterday.

They ate all the berries that way, never taking their eyes off each other. And when the ritual was over, Flannigan stepped back and acted as if none of it had mattered. Tess brought her own racing heart under control and pretended she didn't care. She could eat strawberries with anybody she wanted to—in exactly that way, with berry-flavored lips touching, sharing the sweetness.

To show him she didn't care, she ate all her breakfast, every crumb, never backing down from his stare. *Damn, why was he watching her that way?* It reminded her of their courtship days, when she'd be standing on a stage and could feel his eyes all the way across a crowded room. And everywhere his deep blue gaze touched, her body heated up.

Now, it was not only heating up, it was melting, running in a puddle at her feet and flowing across the room toward him. Out of the corner of her eye she saw the bed, looming larger than life, as if their recent loving had invested it with magical powers.

Why didn't he say something? Why didn't she say something? Suddenly she couldn't think of what she could say to this man. Never in her life had she been at a loss for words with Mick Flannigan. Not when they had been friends, then lovers, then husband and wife. Never. And now that they had shared strawberries—and a bed— she couldn't think of a single thing to say.

"How's . . ."

"What about . . ."

They both spoke at the same time. Mick pulled a cigar from his pocket and stuck it between his teeth, unlit.

"Ladies first," he said.

"I'm no lady."

"You're the grandest lady I know."

"Really?" She was as pleased as if he had pinned a medal on her chest. Although she'd never aspired to be a lady, primarily because Aunt Bertha had tried so hard to make her into one, she was inordinately pleased that Mick considered her to be a grand one.

"That you are, Tess, my girl."

He crossed the room and took the black rose from the jar. Then he snipped off the long stem and all the thorns and tucked the rose behind her ear.

"A special rose for a very special lady."

"Mick." She caught his hand and pressed it against her cheek. "Don't make me like you too much."

"Are you liking me, Tess?" He brightened like the newly polished earth after a good soaking rain.

"More than I should."

"By whose rules?"

"Mine." She released his hand and pushed her chair back from the table. Facing him almost nose to nose, as was her habit, she told him the truth.

"Mick, I like the way you look, I like the way you smile, I like the way you make me feel in bed. But I don't like the idea that I might fall in love with you all over again . . . So I'm not going to."

"Good. I'm not going to fall in love with you, either."

Blue eyes clashed with green. Neither of them would back down. It was O'Toole who saved them from their own stubbornness. He got off his perch on the bed and sashayed across the room until he reached his mistress. Then he wound himself between her legs. When she ignored him, he put his paw on her legs and gave an unholy yowl.

She scooped to pick him. "Poor O'Toole." She rubbed her chest and planted small kisses on the top of his head. "Poor lonesome cat. Is everybody ignoring you?" She cuddled him close and rubbed her face against his soft fur. "Don't worry, old darling, I'm not going to let you get lonesome, not for one single minute."

"If I'm ever reincarnated, I'm coming back as a tomcat," said Flannigan, marching toward the door.

"Flannigan," Tess called. He turned, and they glared at each other. "You already are a tomcat."

Eight

Tess and Flannigan took Casey to buy new clothes. They sat on plush-backed chairs in Reed's, the finest department store in Tupelo, watching as Casey paraded in front of them, strutting with his chest puffed out, showing off one new outfit after the other.

"My old clothes are fine," he said, fingering his new twill slacks and striped oxford-cloth shirt. "I don't take charity," he added, preening in front of a three-way mirror.

"This is not charity," Mick insisted. "Consider this an investment. How are Tess and I going to get anybody to claim you if you don't look spiffy? If we don't polish you up some, we'll never get you off our hands."

Casey grinned, then disappeared into the dressing room once more.

"Flannigan, you're going to hurt his feelings."

"Casey and I understand each other." Mick leaned back, pleased with himself. "Besides, didn't you see the look on his face? He hasn't had this much fun in years."

"Neither have you?"

"What?" He swiveled to look at Tess.

"You should see yourself, Mick. You're as proud of that old man as if he were really your father."

"What about you, my girl? I thought I saw a daughterly twinkle in your eye when he modeled those Cuban shorts."

"Bermuda. The shorts were Bermuda."

"I knew it was one of those islands. I'm a blue-jeans man, myself."

They faced forward again, waiting for Casey to return, but neither of them denied their instincts. As Mick thought about it, he decided he *was* having the time of his life. Funny how an ordinary outing to a department store could be more satisfying than flying into a strange city and walking strange streets to see if anything exciting beckoned to him.

Suddenly the thought of flying into yet another town filled him with an odd sort of weariness. Maybe he was getting too old to chase rainbows. Or maybe he just didn't know which rainbow to chase anymore.

Casey returned in a plaid sports coat and linen slacks. They ended up buying him a modest wardrobe, including underwear. He selected an assortment of undershorts featuring Snoopy and Superman and Garfield.

"Do you have some plans there, Casey?" Mick teased.

"Maybe I'm planning to let you borrow them. You're the one who does all the tomcatting."

Tess pretended she didn't hear them. The night in Flannigan's embrace rose up in her, and she suddenly wanted this journey to last forever. Behind her, Mick and Casey laughed and joked and carried on like old friends. She pictured the three of them, climbing into the rented brown Ford and riding west, into the setting sun. She even heard theme music playing—"Ninety-Nine Bottles of Beer on the Wall." She and Flannigan used to sing it whenever they traveled. Maybe they would sing it again.

All of a sudden she felt lighthearted. Turning back to Mick and Casey, she said, "Next stop is the barbershop."

It was afternoon by the time Tess and Mick had Casey ready to travel. Sitting in conference in unit four, they decided to travel by car rather than Mick's plane. The car was Casey's choice, mainly because he fancied the idea of the three of them on the road together.

"On a search like this," he said, "I'm going to have to depend on places to jog my memory. Now, it seems to me I can see places better from the ground than from the air."

"Don't you think we should start our search right here in Tupelo?" Tess asked.

"I've pretty much scoured this area," Casey said. "I thought we might head south, down toward Vicksburg." Vicksburg sounded romantic to him.

"Is there any particular reason you've chosen that city?" Tess was beginning to have a few doubts about the success of their venture, especially with Casey in charge. She glanced to Mick for some help in the matter. He winked at her and blew two smoke rings in her direction.

"It's just a feeling I have." Casey crossed his hands over his heart. "A feeling in my heart."

"Probably indigestion," Mick said. He and Casey laughed. Tess didn't find it all that funny.

"I don't know about you two clowns, but I'm planning to get on the road."

Casey sat back, twirling his gold-tipped cane and smiling as Tess swept from the room. Mick took a long draw on his cigar and watched the door long after she had disappeared.

"Well," Casey finally said, "aren't we going after her?"

"No."

"Why not?"

"She'll be back."

"How do you know?"

"Because she has four suitcases and nobody to carry them. She'll come back in here, smiling that pretty smile of hers, and she'll say, 'Mick, my suitcases need loading.'" He laughed. "I've always enjoyed watching Tess Jones at work."

He took his cigar out and studied its glowing tip. "Besides, I want to finish my cigar before we start toward Vicksburg."

He leaned back and puffed contentedly, thinking of Tess and her four suitcases next door. He loved to feel needed. Although Tess was probably the most independent, free-spirited woman he had ever known, she always made him feel needed.

Next door, Tess gave O'Toole a treat so he would travel without complaint. While he was eating, she put the last few items into her suitcases, and then started out the door to get Mick.

"What in the world are you doing, Tess Jones?" She marched back into her room, still giving herself a lecture. "Next thing you know, you won't even be able to take a bath without Mick Flannigan there to scrub your back."

She picked up the phone and dialed the front desk.

"This is Tess Jones in unit three. Can you send a bellboy to take my bags to the car?"

"A bellboy? Did you say a bellboy?" The man on the other end of the line hooted with laughter.

"That's what I said. I have four, and three of them are extremely heavy."

"Lady, this is not the Beverly Hills Hotel. We don't have bellboys."

Tess gave a fleeting thought to charm or bribery or both, then changed her mind. She'd show that Flannigan. If she didn't miss her guess, he was sitting next door, smoking his cigar and laughing, waiting for her to call him.

"There's more than one way to skin a cat. Pardon my language, O'Toole." She started toward the door. "Wait here," she told her cat. "I'll be right back."

She eased out the door, humming to herself.

Twenty minutes later she pounded on Mick's door.

"Flannigan. Open up."

He winked at Casey. "See. What did I tell you?" Tess was standing in the doorway with the sun in her hair. He lounged against the doorframe, drinking in the sight of her. "You've come for my help, I see."

"Your help? Why, Flannigan. All I have to do is snap my fingers, and at least six men come to do my bidding." Her arms were still sore from lugging her heavy suitcases, but she didn't tell him that. Instead she stepped aside and nodded toward the Ford. The engine was humming, and the door on the driver's side was ajar.

"I came to say that I'm off to Vicksburg, in case you want to come along."

"The car's running."

"I know that. I hot-wired it."

"You hot-wired it?"

"Why should that surprise you? You taught me how." She reached up and pinched his cheek. "Don't be getting any ideas that you're indispensable, Flannigan."

With that final word she pranced off toward the car, looking for all the world like a high-bred, high-strung champion filly.

After Flannigan had finished laughing, he strode after her. She was already sitting behind the wheel, humming along with a blues song that was blaring from the radio.

In one smooth motion he slid under the wheel, lifting and pushing her to the passenger side. Then he slid across and wrapped her in his arms.

"What do you think you're doing?"

He smiled into her eyes. "What do *you* think I'm doing?"

"If you're thinking of love in the afternoon, please remember that this is not your hearse."

"No curtains?" He glanced into the backseat and pretended to be crushed. "I can't tell you how that disappoints me." He held her a fraction of a second longer. "This is not about making love, much as it pains me to disappoint you." Grinning, he moved back under the wheel. "I'm driving."

"Now I know why I liked Carson better than you: He was never bossy."

"Then he was no challenge at all for you. I'll bet you were bored out of your mind." He banged the door shut harder than he had meant to. Not only did he hope Carson had been boring, but also impotent.

With black thoughts racing through his mind, he put the car in reverse and backed out of the parking space. Suddenly he slammed on the brakes.

"What's the matter?" Tess asked.

"We forgot Casey."

"I didn't forget Casey. *You* forgot Casey."

Mick pulled the car back into the parking slot. She sat in the car, holding her heavy hair off her neck as Mick sprinted back into the motel. Not only had they forgotten Casey, they'd forgotten Mick's bag as well. Things were getting out of hand between them. Tess could see that.

"I have to do better than this, O'Toole," she told the cat, who was already drowsing in the sun on the backseat.

Mick disappeared briefly into the motel room, and while he was out of sight, Tess changed her mind about how she could deal with him. It had all been well and good to stand in an empty motel room and vow she could go to his bed as many times as she liked and not lose her heart. That had been before the strawberries and the silver platter and the single black rose tucked into her hair. That had been before he had declared her to be the grandest lady of all.

"Ahh, Flannigan." She sighed, watching as he came out the door with his duffel bag in one hand and Casey in tow. "You never lost an ounce of your charm, did you?"

Mick was laughing at something Casey was saying. Tess's heart climbed up into her throat, and tears gathered behind her eyelids.

"Don't make me wish for things I can't have, Flannigan," she whispered. "Don't make me want you and Casey to be *real*."

The two men disappeared behind the car to stow their bags in the trunk. What was she doing sitting in a car headed to Vicksburg, Mississippi, with one man she didn't dare love and another man she wasn't sure she could trust?

"Ready?" Mick slid back into the driver's seat, and Casey settled in beside O'Toole.

"Ready," she said, never turning her head to look at him. Somehow it seemed important not to look at him now that they were actually on the road, going to a specific destination. They used to love traveling together.

She was determined that this trip would *not* be another nostalgic journey into the past.

Afternoon traffic was heavy, so she didn't talk while Mick drove across town to the Natchez Trace Parkway. When he was on that lonely and beautiful stretch of scenic road, she leaned her head against the back of the seat and closed her eyes.

"Sleepy?" Mick asked.

"Yes." She didn't look at him.

He drove a while in silence.

"You can put your head on my shoulder," he said at last.

"No, thank you."

"I just thought you might be more comfortable that way."

He watched her out of the corner of his eye, admiring the way her skin looked in the sunshine pouring through the window. Like soft, ripe peaches. He was hungry just looking at her.

He was selfish, he decided, selfish right down to the cockles of his broken heart. It had broken his heart to leave her ten years ago, and it was breaking his heart to know he had to leave her again. But in spite of all that, in spite of knowing he would walk away when all this business with Casey was over, he still wanted her. Damn his selfish hide, he wanted to touch her skin, to feel her in his arms. And yes, he wanted to make love to her. Now. He wanted to pull the car off the road and take her into one of the secluded groves along the Trace and strip her bare and worship her body just as he had done last night.

His early morning burst of nobility was wearing thin. Now that he'd had a taste of her, he couldn't even get through one day without aching at the mere sight of her. How in the hell he was going to get through the next few days without going to her bed again was a mystery to him.

His hands tightened on the wheel. He had to. He had to leave Tess Jones alone.

"Casey," he said softly, so as not to awaken Tess. There was no answer. "Casey," he said again, glancing into the rearview mirror. Casey was fast asleep, his head thrown back and his mouth working in silent snores, like a fish.

Mick was accustomed to traveling alone, with only the noise of the airplane engine to keep him company. In the early days of his gadding about, he had enjoyed his solitude. Lately it had been a lonely way to travel. Now, with no one to talk to, he waited for the lonely feeling to come.

But it didn't. Mile after mile of the Natchez Trace passed by. Mick played the radio with the volume turned down low, tapping his fingers on the steering wheel when the rhythm was especially lively. Occasionally he glanced in the mirror to check on Casey. But more often he looked at the sleeping beauty by his side.

How could a man feel lonely when he was transporting precious cargo? He clicked off the radio and began to sing, softly, in a deep, rich baritone.

"Ninety-nine bottles of beer on the wall, ninety-nine bottles of beer. Take one down and pass it around, ninety-eight bottles of beer on the wall. . . . ninety-eight bottles . . ."

" . . .of beer on the wall," Tess chimed in.

"You're awake," he said, turning to smile at her.

"You were singing my song."

"*Our* traveling song."

"I didn't think you'd remember."

"I could never forget."

His eyes held hers a fraction longer; then he faced the road. They were silent for a while as memories washed over them. And then Tess began to sing once more.

"Ninety-eight bottles of beer."

He joined in. "Take one down and pass it around, ninety-seven bottles of beer on the wall."

By the time they got to fifty bottles of beer on the wall, Casey was awake. He added his lilting Irish tenor to the song. When they finally got to one bottle and the end of the song, Tess declared the three of them could go onstage as a trio.

"You could join my act," she said.

"You're a performer, my dear?" Casey asked.

"She's the best blues singer in the world," Mick said.

"Pay no attention. He exaggerates." But Tess was secretly pleased. If Mick kept pinning medals on her, she was going to think he really did like her, just the way she was. That was foolish, of course. If he had thought she was all that great, he never would have left her in the first place.

"Is anybody getting hungry?" Mick asked.

Tess and Casey agreed that all that singing had made them ravenous. Mick stopped in Kosciusko to buy food, and the three of them had a picnic beside the Trace in a shaded glen with a clear stream meandering through the trees. O'Toole gave up his regal posture long enough to try his paw at fishing.

" 'Tis the best meal I've ever had," Casey declared, casting the remnants of his bologna sandwich to the birds. Two mockingbirds and a cardinal ate the crumbs, then flew into the branches of an oak tree and began to sing.

"Excuse me," Casey said as he trailed along behind the birds. When he was standing under their tree, he picked up a stick and began to conduct nature's orchestra.

Tess watched for a while, then turned to Mick.

"He's a professional."

"How do you know?"

"He's had training. See how he wields that stick, like a baton."

"Tess . . ." He started to tell about Casey, and then he paused, studying her face. It was alight with dreams. What was the use of telling her the truth about Casey now and spoiling her fun? He'd let her have one more day. He'd let *all* of them have one more day of make-believe.

"What, Mick?"

"Nothing." He stood up and began to clear away the picnic trash. "I suppose we should be moving on."

Tess stood for a moment, watching Casey. He was having the time of his life, humming and waving his imaginary baton, his legs white and skinny in his brand-new madras-plaid Bermuda shorts.

"I'm going to miss that old man when we find his son," she said.

"So will I."

They loaded the car and set off down the Natchez Trace once more. By the time they arrived in Vicksburg, it was after dark.

Casey rolled down his car window. "Smell that river. I always did want to walk up and down the banks of the Mississippi, watching the riverboats and listening to the sound of their whistles."

"We'll do that," Tess said, "but our main priority will be the search for your son."

"Of course."

The passing glare of headlights allowed Casey to catch Mick's eye in the rearview mirror. Neither of them felt too noble at the moment.

They checked into a motel by the river. And afterward, the three of them strolled beside the Mississippi, arms linked, listening to the rush of water and the far-off cry of boat whistles as barges plowed their way south toward the Gulf.

Eventually Casey pleaded old age, and sat on a bench while Mick and Tess walked on down the river. They were holding hands. Casey considered that a good sign.

He leaned on his gold-tipped cane and looked out across the singing waters.

"A selfish, lying old man I'm being, but God, just give me this one little miracle. One miracle, and then I'll not be askin' you for more."

When the moon was tracking across the skies and Casey was snoring in his very own room, Tess arose from her bed and went to the window. She pressed her forehead against the cool glass pane and looked out into the darkness.

Mick would not come for her tonight. She knew that. He wouldn't pick her lock, and she wouldn't awaken with him in her arms. She stared out the window a while, seeing nothing except endless blackness. That's how she felt inside right now. Darkness that went on forever and ever. Night without end.

She turned from the window and hugged her arms around herself.

"What am I going to do, O'Toole?"

O'Toole burrowed his head deeper into his fur, ignoring her.

Tess left the window and walked toward the bathroom light. The lonesome blues fell so heavily on her that her shoulders stooped under the weight. Light from the bathroom spilled onto the vanity, and she dug into her traveling case until she found what she wanted: a single black rose, pressed between the pages of a slim volume of poetry by Yeats. Irish poetry.

She held the fragile rose against her cheek and began to read aloud, softly.

Her eyes skimmed down the rest of the poem, and she read of the poet's longing to be where "peace comes dropping slow." She closed the little book, pressing the rose back between the pages.

"Is this what your brooding Irish soul wants, Mick Flannigan? Is this why you left me? So you can find peace in solitude?"

She replaced the book, remembering how Mick had held her hand as they walked beside the river, with his fingers twined in hers and his warm palm sending out a steady heat.

Suddenly she saw a vision of the future, with Mick spinning out his lonely years in a cabin in a glen, and her standing in the spotlights on an empty stage. She slid her robe from her shoulders, letting the feathers trail along the carpet. Then she left her gown in a pile on a chair.

She put on black jogging shorts and a black tank top, and let herself out the door, not even bothering with shoes. Outside, the night was warm and damp with mists rising from the river. Her footsteps fell softly on the grass.

There were no lights inside Flannigan's room. She picked the lock and eased open the door.

Nine

"Your red hair gives you away."

Her eyes adjusted to the darkness, and Tess saw Mick, sitting in a chair across the room.

"Don't you know it's dangerous to come inside a man's room in the middle of night?"

She didn't say anything, but stood with her hands crossed in front of her chest, watching him. He was shirtless and shoeless. A bottle of scotch sat on the table, and he held a half-empty glass in his hand.

"Drinking alone, Mick?"

"I'm not alone: I have my thoughts to keep me company."

"Are they good company?"

She glided into the room, going as far as the end of the bed.

"They are the devil, straight from the pits of hell."

He was tense. She could tell by the way he held himself and the way his muscles bunched across the top of his shoulders.

With her eyes grown accustomed to the dark,

they watched each other, wary. He was the first to break the silence.

"What brings you here, Tess?"

Not *Tess, my girl*, she noticed. Merely Tess. Mick Flannigan was in a black mood to match her own. She advanced toward him, slowly.

"Do you want the truth," she asked, "or do you want me to make up a pretty lie?"

"The truth will do."

"I'm lonesome, Mick."

She was standing so close now, her legs were practically touching his knees. His blue eyes looked almost black as he gazed up at her. Then, suddenly, he set his glass aside and held out his arms. She went to him.

He drew her onto his lap and cuddled her close.

"Tess . . . Tess, my girl," he whispered into her hair.

She wound one arm around his neck and pressed her face against his chest. Her lips grazed his skin, and he shivered. His arms tightened around her, and she could feel the steady thrum of his heart under her cheek.

"I was standing at my window," she whispered, "and I thought of the empty years ahead, Mick." A tear trembled on her lash, then fell softly onto his chest.

"It's all right. I'm here."

"But you won't be. Not always." He didn't deny her words, and another tear wet his skin. "Suddenly, Mick, I was lonesome beyond enduring."

They clung to each other, mute with longing. He smoothed her silky hair, over and over. Then he began to sing, "Too-ra-loo-ra-loo-ral."

His rich baritone voice filled the silence. "Hush now, don't you cry."

She hugged him tightly, comforted by his arms

and the words of "The Irish Lullaby." When he finished the first verse, she lifted her face to his.

"That's beautiful, Mick. Don't stop."

He continued singing, swaying a little, rocking her in his embrace. And as they had in years gone by when Mick had held her in his arms, her blues crept back into the shadows, and a gentle sense of peace stole over her.

Her eyelids drooped, and her head nodded. He looked down at her, humming softly as she drifted into sleep.

"Sleep well, my darling," he whispered. "Sweet dreams."

Balancing her carefully, he reached for his harmonica, being careful not to waken her.

Lifting the blues harp to his mouth, he played "The Irish Lullaby" softly, ever so softly. The haunting notes filled the emptiness. "Hush now, don't you cry," the harmonica sang into the darkness.

Mick finished that tune and played another. Once he thought of carrying Tess to his bed and tucking her in, but he was too selfish to let her go. She had come to him and climbed into his lap with complete trust. He would hold her and protect her and comfort her until morning came, and then she would awaken slowly, as she always did, and know that he had been there for her all night long.

It was the very least he could do; for tomorrow he would say good-bye.

Tess felt stiff. She yawned and stretched, and encountered a very solid chest. Her eyes flew open.

"Good morning, Tess, my girl. Did you sleep well?"

Mick was still in his chair and she was still in his lap, exactly as she had been last night. He smiled down at her, but he looked drawn and weary, exactly as a man who had missed a night's sleep should.

"Is it morning?"

"Almost. I can see a slice of dawn through the curtains."

"Have I been here all night? Like this?"

"Yes."

"You held me all night long?"

"Yes."

She drew a ragged breath. Then she put her hands tenderly on his face, tracing the lines of fatigue she saw there.

"Mick Flannigan, you always were my best friend in the whole wide world."

"Past tense?"

Her fingers played lightly over his face, lingering longest on his lips.

"Sometimes I think you still are." She reached up and kissed him. It was a gentle kiss, given with a heart full of gratitude.

He smiled. "Do you feel better this morning, Tess, my girl?"

"Enormously. Tremendously." Her face was radiant with a smile as she rose from his lap. Her legs were a little stiff, and he caught her arm when she wobbled.

"You're like a newborn colt."

She leaned down and nuzzled her cheek against his.

"And you're like a great warm blanket. Only better."

He put his arms around her, holding her close for a moment, and then he let her go. She stepped back.

"Mick . . ." His eyes, bluer than the lakes of Ireland, lifted to meet hers. She held her breath, drowning, drowning and not wanting to come to the surface. Then she wet her lips with the tip of her tongue and gathered her courage to leave. "Thank you for last night."

"You're more than welcome. It was my gift to you."

Your going-away gift? she wanted to ask. But she didn't, for her heart already knew the answer.

"It's a gift I will treasure. Always." *Long after you're gone.* She lifted her hand in a sassy salute, then turned and started toward the door.

He watched her all the way across the room, then he said, "See you at breakfast."

With her hand on the doorknob, she turned back to him.

"You must be very tired. Why don't you sleep and let me handle Casey this morning."

"No, thank you. There will be plenty of time to sleep."

After you're gone, she thought. The blues threatened to swamp her once more, but she pushed them away. She had to be invincible, just a little while longer.

"Then I'll see you at breakfast."

She gave a jaunty wave and went out the door.

Mick rubbed his hand over his eyes. His head felt blurred, inside and out. He sat in his chair a while longer with his eyes closed and his head bowed.

"I must be a fool," he said. Then he lifted his head and rose from his chair. "But a noble one."

The three of them spent all morning in Vicksburg, following Casey's whims. He visited two old men, living down by the riverfront, who, according to Casey, used to know the whereabouts of his son.

Tess and Mick waited for him in the car, and when he came back, he reported that their memories had grown dim with age.

"Perhaps we should hire a private investigator," Tess said. "Or contact some of the orphanages and welfare agencies in this area."

Mick turned to the backseat and scrutinized Casey with intense blue eyes.

"Casey, what do *you* think we should do?"

"A different city we should be going to, I'm thinkin'." Casey watched Mick closely for resistance, and when he didn't see any, he continued. "Maybe we should head south . . . we love traveling together so."

"Mick," Tess said, her eyes sparkling, "let's go to the Gulf Coast."

Mick couldn't resist the temptation. He had planned to say good-bye today, but seeing Tess with happiness shining on her face, he decided to stay one more day, only one. And then he'd say good-bye.

And so they headed south, singing their traveling song and laughing. Tess, sitting on the front seat harmonizing with Mick, didn't know why she had suggested the Gulf Coast. It held too many memories for them. Was she trying to recapture the past? She knew the past could neither be recaptured nor changed. Perhaps she was only trying to postpone the parting. It was coming— soon. She could feel Mick slipping away from her, already putting distance between them.

They reached the coast by eight o'clock. The first thing they saw as they drove along Highway 90 between Gulfport and Biloxi was the colorful big top of a carnival. Mick slowed the car, peering into the evening darkness.

"Can you see the name, Tess?"

"Not yet. I can see the lights just up ahead. Wait, Mick! It's Brinkley Brothers' Carnival!"

"So it is," he said, driving on by the big top. All his life he had tried to move forward. Sometimes he had gone sideways and sometimes he hadn't moved at all, but he didn't want to move backward. He'd already done enough traveling backward this past weekend to shred his heart to pieces. He didn't want any more trips into the past.

Tess swiveled her head to study him, but she didn't say anything. She knew what the carnival had meant to him. It had been more than a shelter, more than a way of life: it had been his home. She reached across the seat and squeezed his hand. He didn't turn but she could see the corners of his mouth turn up in a smile.

"I'm thinkin' a carnival would be fun," Casey said from the backseat. The carnival was also romantic. At least, that's what Casey thought. And he was about to run out of ideas for romance. Time was running short, and he was getting desperate.

When Mick didn't stop the car and turn around, Casey tried again.

"When I was a little boy, I always wanted to go to the carnival."

"Didn't you ever get to?" Tess asked.

"Alas, my family was too strict. They said it was the devil's playground."

"So it was." Mick chuckled. "And I was one of the devils."

"You know carnivals?" Casey leaned over the seat.

"I grew up in one. That very carnival, as a matter of fact. Brinkley Brothers' Carnival."

"Saints be praised. We'll be turning back then, going to pay a visit to the folks who gave you your raising, or I'll be missin' my guess. And besides that, I've been wanting some cotton candy. My mouth is fairly watering for the taste of some pink cotton candy."

"Your mouth is fairly watering from talking too much," Mick said, but he was laughing as he turned the car around and headed back to the carnival.

The first thing they did was buy some cotton candy. As Mick stood in the midway with colored lights flashing all around and the voices of hawkers ringing in his ears, he was transported backward to a time when he was twelve years old.

Uncle Arthur was fitting a suit on him, wielding scissors and needle and thread with an expertness born of necessity. "Hold still, Mick. I've got to get this right." Uncle Arthur had cut up an old red polka-dotted shirt he wore sometimes when he subbed for Grady the Clown, and he was trying to fashion a bow tie for Mick.

"Now remember this," he had said. "Most things in life you can get with a good con. But the things that are really worth having, you have to earn." He worked some more on the tie, cutting and measuring until he had made a lopsided but passable tie. "Now we're going in there together, Mick, and we're going to convince Mr. Buzz Brinkley that you can earn your keep here at the carnival and that you won't be hardly any trouble at all and won't cost the Brinkley brothers a penny. And then me and you will be a team, hey? We're going to earn that right to be, hey?"

Mick stood on the midway with Tess and O'Toole on one side and Casey on the other, hearing the voice from his past.

"Mick." Tess tugged his hand, bringing him back to the present. "Look, Mick. There's a fortune-telling booth." She leaned around and smiled at Casey. "Do you want to have your fortune told?"

"You kids go on and have a good time. O'Toole and I are going to sit on that bench over there and eat my cotton candy and watch the crowds. Then maybe we'll take a little stroll down the midway to see all the attractions. We'll be waiting for you on the bench." Having said all that, he strolled off, swinging O'Toole's carrying case and whistling.

Mick and Tess stood side by side, watching him go. A large gang of noisy teenagers passed close by, jostling Tess aside so that she fell against Mick. He caught her close to his chest, and they stared at each other, frozen in time, as red and blue and yellow neon lights played over their faces.

"Do you want to know what the future holds for you, Tess, my girl?"

"Do you?"

"I already know mine." His eyes took on a bleak faraway look.

"You're leaving, aren't you, Mick?"

"How did you know?"

"I felt it. You started leaving yesterday, as we walked beside the river."

"It's time to be moving on."

"What about Casey?"

"I'll find a place for him."

"No. He can come with me. Back to Chicago."

"He doesn't have a son, you know."

"I suspected as much."

"He's just a lonely old man without a family."

"Then he and I will divide our loneliness so we're both only half-lonely."

"Are you lonely, Tess, my girl?"

"Right now I am." She was bleak, too, but she tossed her head and gave him a bright smile. "It will pass. Someone will come along to fill the void. Who knows? Maybe I'll marry again."

Flannigan wanted to roar like a wounded jungle beast. But he had no right.

"Perhaps you will." He caressed her cheek with the back of his hand. "I hope you'll find happiness the next time around."

"It's not happiness I'm looking for, Flannigan. I'm already happy most of the time."

"What are you looking for?"

"Somebody who can tolerate my wicked ways and stick around for the long haul."

Flannigan didn't want to think of another man staying with Tess for the long haul, growing old with her, perhaps having children, eventually dying and being buried by her side or else having their ashes mixed and tossed into a shining river somewhere. But he had no right to voice any objections. He was only an ex-husband, passing through.

"What about you, Flannigan? What are you looking for?"

"I'll know when I find it."

They stood holding each other in the midway with the crowd swirling around them.

"Hey, big fella," a hawker yelled at Flannigan. "Are you going to stand there hugging your girl, or are you going to win her a teddy bear?"

"Win me a teddy bear, Mick. Something to keep me warm at night until I can find another husband." Tess stepped back from him, laughing and sparkling for all she was worth. She was determined to be merry and amusing and, above all, indestructible. Mick was leaving, as she had known he would, and this time, she was going to tell him good-bye.

Her heart could break when she got back to

Chicago, and she could pour out her anguish in a smoky nightclub, singing the blues. But while she was with Mick Flannigan tonight, she was going to be Tess Jones, the woman with an invincible spirit.

Mick pitched nickels into a bottle and won her a teddy bear. Then he knocked weighted targets off a shelf with a baseball and won her a gold pasteboard crown. They rode the carousel and the Ferris wheel and the trains through the tunnel of love, laughing as they had when they were young and falling in love. When they came to a booth with plastic ducks swimming across fake water, Mick shot them down, one by one, and won her another prize. It was a fake diamond ring.

Yellow neon lights set the glass stone sparkling, and for an instant Tess imagined the ring was real. She glanced up to see a dark, brooding look on Flannigan's face. That would never do. *This* time, she was going to be in charge of the good-byes. She was determined that they remember each other with laughter and not with tears.

"It's an omen, Mick." She laughed, and held the ring out to him. "Put it on my finger."

He slipped the ring on her finger, catching her lighthearted mood.

"Will you marry me, Tess Jones?"

"Only if your name is not Flannigan or Carson or O'Toole. I've tried all of them, and they didn't last."

"The name is Canfield, Raiford Canfield." He gave an exaggerated bow from the waist.

"In that case, Mr. Canfield, I accept."

He squeezed her hand and stood looking down into her face, wishing they were twenty-four again and starting all over. The intensity of his mood tugged at her, and she struggled against it. In spite of her valiant efforts, she couldn't recapture her lighthearted spirit.

"Don't do this to me, Mick," she whispered. He leaned closer, his dark hair falling over his forehead. She reached up to smooth it back. "Don't make this hard."

He cupped her face with both hands. "I love you, Tess, my girl. I'll always love you."

"I know . . . but not enough to stay."

He pressed his lips to her forehead. They stood that way for a long time, and then Tess pulled back to look up at him.

"Mick, take me to a motel."

"Are you sleepy?"

"No. I want to tell you good-bye."

"Tess . . ."

She knew he was going to protest. Damn his noble hide, he was going to walk away without so much as a decent kiss.

"Don't you dare say a single thing, Mick Flannigan. Don't you dare take this away from me."

"Take what away from you?"

"The chance to tell you good-bye, dammit." Her cheeks flamed as her temper flared. "The last time you walked out on me, I didn't get a chance for so much as a good-bye kiss. For weeks I kept thinking you'd come back. It seemed as if you'd just gone down to the corner grocery store and had somehow lost your way."

"I'm sorry. So sorry."

"I don't want to hear how sorry you are, Flannigan. I just want to tell you good-bye properly this time. And when I'm finished with you, you'll know I've said good-bye forever."

"Forever sounds so final."

"It is, Flannigan. Our paths crossed this time by

chance, and I'm going to make damned certain they don't cross again."

He didn't have to ask why: He knew. Saying good-bye was too hard to do.

"Let's go." He took her hand and practically dragged her through the crowd.

As tall as she was, she had to hurry to keep up with him. Casey was waiting for them on the bench, his face fixed in an expectant smile. When he saw them, his smile faded. He had wanted to see two people who had fallen in love all over again, but what he saw was two people who looked as if they were heading into the Battle of Armageddon.

He stood up, leaning a little on his cane. "Did you two enjoy the carnival?"

"Marvelous."

"Wonderful."

They both spoke at once, their grim voices sounding as if they were describing germ warfare. Casey's heart was heavy as he followed them to the car, trotting to keep up.

"I'm guessing my little game's about over," he said, but nobody heard him.

They all climbed into the car, Casey sitting in the back with O'Toole. Of the four of them, only O'Toole was in a good mood.

The car roared down Highway 90, carrying its four passengers and its black cloud of gloom. Mick stopped at the first motel he saw, a small grouping of adobe cottages set back from the highway among live-oak trees shrouded with Spanish moss.

He made quick work of checking them in and helping settle Casey into his room. When he came out of Casey's room, Tess had already disappeared into hers. He stalked toward his own door, his thoughts as thunderous as the storms that swept over the Irish Sea.

What was she doing now? Probably plotting her outrageous plans for saying good-bye. She was going to come to his bed, was she? Come to his bed and weave her magic spell around him and then leave forever, was she?

"We'll see about that, Tess Jones Flannigan Carson O'Toole."

He spun around and stormed toward her room. He didn't even bother knocking.

The first thing he noticed after he'd picked her lock and eased through the door was her gold-sequined shoes, one on top of the dresser and one tossed on the bed. The next thing he saw was a collection of silk gowns, spread upon the bed in a bright rainbow of color.

The shower was running, and a cloud of steam came through the bathroom door. Following a trail of feathers and jasmine fragrance, he made his relentless way toward Tess. O'Toole, who had claimed a red gown for his own, glanced up from his nest of silk, then curled back into a ball and shut his eyes.

Flannigan pulled back the curtain and stepped into the shower.

Tess paused in the act of soaping her chest, and turned around. The soap and the washcloth slid slowly out of her hands.

"My God. Flannigan." She looked him up and down, starting at the top of his head and ending at his feet. "You're wearing boots."

"I always say good-bye with my boots on."

He caught her around the waist and hauled her into his body. Soap-slick skin collided with wet blue jeans. Her eyes widened.

"You're crazy."

"You're the one who wanted to say good-bye."

His mouth slammed down on hers in a savage

kiss. She struggled against him, beating his back with her fists. He held on to her, kissing her relentlessly. She flailed and clawed his back, at the same time opening her mouth to welcome his ravaging tongue.

"Oh, Flannigan . . . Flannigan."

He backed her against the shower wall, bracing his hands on either side of her shoulders. Then he bent down so his mouth was only inches from hers.

"When I've finished with you, you'll know I've said good-bye forever." His voice had dropped to the deep low octave that always signaled trouble. She heard the rattling of sabers, smelled the burning of gunpowder. "Isn't that what you said, Tess?"

"I said it. I also said I was going to give you a proper good-bye."

"How proper?" He eased back, and she heard the metallic whisper of his zipper, saw the brief struggle with his wet jeans. Her heart pounded in her chest. "This proper?" he added.

Suddenly he lifted her up, and she was astraddle him with her legs wrapped around his hips and her back against the wall. Thunder met lightning. The clash sent O'Toole scurrying under the bed.

Love and pain and rage boiled in Flannigan as he thundered into Tess, and he cried out his feelings in a heavy Gaelic tongue. She clung to him, calling his name over and over until it was both litany of praise and blues melody of a breaking heart.

The water cascaded onto them, unheeded. Soap melted and ran in a white puddle down the drain. Flannigan kept his footing by sheer force of will. His clothes were drenched, and Tess's breasts were pink where his shirt buttons pressed into her tender flesh.

The battle raged on and on, and still they couldn't say good-bye. They devoured each other, hips joined in a dance as old as time and mouths pressed together, open and hungry.

They held on, not wanting to let go, not wanting the loving to end. But finally they could hold back no longer. He shouted her name, and it echoed around the tile walls, a long, drawn-out lament.

She laid her forehead against his shoulder, not knowing whether it was water or tears she dripped over his shirt. He cupped the back of her head, and pressed her close.

They stayed that way for a long while, holding on to each other in silent agony. And finally he let her go. He lowered her gently to her feet. She leaned against the wall for support, waiting and watching.

His eyes looked like blue bottle glass that had been shattered. They never left hers as he rearranged his wet clothes. The only sounds were his labored breathing and the water that continued to fall around them.

Say something! Tess screamed silently.

But he didn't. He kept looking at her with shattered eyes.

She started to speak. She even opened her mouth, but suddenly she knew there was nothing else to say.

Flannigan watched her awhile longer. Then he reached out one hand and tenderly traced her face, starting at her eyebrows and ending with her lips.

She closed her eyes, memorizing the feel of his hand on her wet skin. Suddenly his touch was gone. She kept her eyes closed, squeezing them tightly to hold back the tears. She heard the rustle of the shower curtain and the squish of water in his boots. Then there was no sound except the rush of water.

And when she opened her eyes, Flannigan was gone. She turned off the water, wrapped herself in a towel, and lay down on her bed, in the middle of her rainbow of silk gowns.

She stared into the darkness for a long, long time. O'Toole hopped onto the bed and sat beside her shoulder. When she didn't acknowledge him, he marched across her and burrowed into the red silk.

"Good-bye, Flannigan," Tess whispered as she turned her face to the dark wall and closed her eyes.

Ten

When Flannigan got back to his room, he stripped off his wet clothes and lay on his bed naked, staring at the dark ceiling. He must have dozed, for eventually the dawn light peeped through his curtains, and he came instantly alert.

The first thing he did was call the airport; the next thing he did was ring Casey's room.

"We need to talk, Casey."

"When?"

"Now. There's a small coffee shop beside the front office. Meet me there."

Flannigan dressed quickly and was already holding a steaming cup of coffee when Casey walked in.

"You look like hell," said Casey, sliding into the booth.

"Good. That's how I feel."

"Where are your boots?"

"Wet." Flannigan didn't explain; he just shifted his tennis shoes out of the way of Casey's cane and handed him a menu. "We'll order first."

After they had ordered, Flannigan began to talk.

"The search for your son is over. I told Tess the truth last night."

"That's best, I'm thinkin'. I was going to tell her myself today." He sopped his biscuit in his egg, watching Flannigan. "I guess I can be finding me another little house down here, something that won't get soggy every time it rains."

"Tess wants to take you with her to Chicago."

Casey underwent a transformation. His face brightened, his shoulders straightened, even his spare frame seemed to fill out.

"Saints be praised."

"You will go with her," said Flannigan, leaning across the table, his face fierce. "You will be charming and cooperative and *good* to her, and you will *never* try to con her again. Is that clear?"•

"Perfectly."

"Good." Flannigan pulled an airplane ticket out of his pocket and placed it on the table. "Here's Tess's ticket. I've made arrangements for it to be changed so she will fly out of Biloxi instead of Tupelo. Yours will be waiting for you at the ticket counter. A taxi will be here at eleven to pick you up."

"How did you get her ticket?"

"I picked her pocket."

"And where will you be going, Mick Flannigan?"

"Somewhere where there are no women with red hair and no old Irish con men."

Casey twirled his cane round and round, studying the tormented man sitting across the table. At last he spoke.

"I wasted most of my life before I found me a family. And then it dropped into my lap by chance. If I hadn't overheard you in the park . . . and if Tess hadn't come back, I would still be in Tupelo in my cardboard box." Casey leaned across the table, his wrinkled face earnest with feeling. "Don't you be waiting a lifetime to find a family, Mick."

"I'm not looking for one."

"What are you looking for?"

"I don't know anymore." He stood up and held out his hand. "Good-bye, Casey. Take care of Tess for me."

Flannigan walked out without looking back. Even saying good-bye to Casey was hard. As he climbed into the rented Ford, he decided that he was getting old, too old to handle greetings and partings. Maybe he would fly back to Tupelo and get his Skyhawk and fly off somewhere in the desert where nothing except jackrabbits and an occasional rattler would keep him company. The way he was feeling now, he would be good company for a rattlesnake.

He drove along the beach, going nowhere in particular. His only purpose was to stay away from the motel until Tess and Casey had gone. Cowardly. That's what he was.

He parked on a deserted section, then pulled off his shoes and walked across the sand, toward the water. The sun beat down on him, beaming hotter as the day progressed. And when it was coming straight down, burning the top of his head, Flannigan looked up.

A jet was lifting into the sky, its engines a dull roar, its contrail blooming white as it made a graceful turn and headed north.

"Good-bye, Tess, my girl."

Flannigan sank onto the sand and watched the water beat against the shore.

Flannigan stayed a week in Biloxi, roaming the beaches alone, looking out across the water and brooding. At night he sat in the back of one smoky piano bar after another, nursing a glass of scotch and listening to the keyboard tinkle out the lonesome blues. He wondered about Tess and Casey. What were they doing now? Were they singing Irish songs? Were they walking along Lake Michigan, with Casey twirling his cane and Tess laughing? It seemed he could hear the sound of her laughter, rising bright and sparkly just underneath the sounds of the piano.

Suddenly he could endure the music no longer. He left his glass of scotch, untouched, and returned to the rented car. It was time to be moving on. Time to stop brooding and start moving forward again. He'd stood still far too long.

He turned the car back toward the adobe motel. Up ahead, the lights of the carnival beckoned to him. He slowed the car, looking at the lights blinking in the darkness. His hand tightened on the wheel, and then he was making a right turn, heading to Brinkley Brothers' Carnival.

A sense of *déjà vu* overtook him, and he felt as if he were coming home. That was foolish, of course. Uncle Arthur was long since dead. And he hadn't kept in touch with the others—Macky, the clown, and his wife, Lisa, the trapeze artist; Joseph, the elephant tamer, and Glen, the Daring Man Shot from the Cannon. Where were they now? Were they all dead? Or were they still here in the midst of the sawdust and the greasepaint and the cotton candy and the tarnished spangles?

He parked the car and started toward the bright lights of the carnival. First he walked, then he began to jog, and finally he broke into a run. But he wasn't running toward the midway, toward booths of stuffed bears and the hot-dog vendors and the crowds of people; he was skirting around the edges, running toward the patched canvas tents that served as dressing rooms, dining rooms, and homes for the people who followed the carnival.

His footsteps slowed as he came to an area where the elephants were chained. Uncle Arthur had told him never to do anything that would excite the elephants.

"Mick." He turned toward the sound of the voice. An old man, stooped under the weight of two buckets, stepped into Mick's path. "Mick Flannigan. Is that you?"

"Joseph?" Mick studied the old man, looking for signs of the younger, more virile man who had handled the elephants as if they were nothing more than housebroken kittens. Joseph's dark hair had turned gray, and his face was seamed with age; but his eyes were the same, as black as two raisins on a cake.

"Joseph, it's you." Mick caught he old man in a bear hug, causing water from the buckets to slosh over both of them. "I never thought I'd see you again."

"I don't know why not. We're your family. A man never forgets his family."

Joseph set down the buckets and took Mick's arm. "You're just in time for supper."

Joseph led him into a sprawling tent. It was the same mess tent Mick remembered. Patches had been added over the years to hold it together, but the side flaps were tied up to let in the evening breeze, and the mingled smells of cabbage and sausage and ripe tomatoes hung in the air, just as they had so many years ago.

When Mick stepped into the tent, a chorus of voices rang out in welcome. People from all over the tent rose from their places at the table and converged on him—Macky was there, wearing his bulbous red nose, and his wife, Lisa, still trim and erect, walking gracefully in the ballet shoes she wore everywhere. Others from his past were there, the dog trainers, a couple of old roustabouts, the leader of the band, and Natasha, the little Gypsy fortune-teller.

They all began talking at once, and gradually Mick caught up on the doings of his carnival family. Glen had left for another carnival, and was still being shot from a cannon daily. Some of the others he knew had moved on, and some had died.

"Come and sit by my side." Natasha took Mick's hand and led him to a table. "Tell us all about your travels."

Mick laughed. "How do you know I've been traveling?"

"Because that was one of your dreams. You used to run to my tent with your dark curls bouncing and your blue eyes shining, yelling, 'Natasha, come out and see this.' And you'd be holding Arthur's old Atlas in your hand, pointing to some faraway spot like Mexico City or Montreal. And you'd say, 'Someday I'm going there, Natasha. I'm going to have my own airplane, and I'm going to fly high above the carnival and wave when I go by.'"

Mick remembered. "I've been to those place, Natasha. In my own airplane."

She squeezed his hand, looking deep into his eyes. Suddenly he remembered another dream, one he'd told only to Sasha. She was remembering too. He could tell by the way her eyes glowed in the center. She leaned closer to him, peering into his eyes, her hands holding tightly to his.

But she didn't say anything. She didn't ask, "What about the rest of your dream, Mick? What have you done about that?"

He had the eerie feeling that Natasha really was a fortune-teller, and that right now she was seeing not only his future but also his past. He didn't shift away from her scrutiny.

There was a waiting stillness around them, a respect always accorded the carnival's oldest, most revered member. At last Natasha released his hand and began to eat her soup.

There was a collective sigh from the watchers, partly of relief, partly of disappointment. They never knew what Sasha would do or say, but she was always good for a show.

"Are you going to stay for the last performance?" Joseph asked Mick.

"He's staying." Natasha never looked up from her soup as she spoke.

"I'll stay."

His old friends pressed him to have supper, and he obliged. Afterward, he let them escort him to the best seat under the big top.

The trumpets blared, the ringmaster came on, and the show began. Funny how age took none of the magic from the circus. Too soon it was over, and long after the crowd had gone, Mick continued to sit in the bleachers, the smells of sawdust and parched peanuts and buttered popcorn drifting around him.

He looked out across the big top at the empty rigging, still swaying as if Lisa were swinging there, and all the dreams of his youth came washing over him.

The carnival had given him a taste for travel and excitement and adventure, and it had never left him; but he'd had another dream too. "Someday," he had said to Natasha, "I'm going to have a family of my own, a *real* family, with a wife and children and a little house that I can always come back to."

In his hell-bent-for-leather pursuit of adventure, he'd lost sight of part of his dream. For ten years he'd traveled the world, restless, always searching, and always coming up empty-handed. Suddenly he knew why. The thing he had been looking for was the thing he'd left behind: love, family, home, children. He'd had all that in Tess and had been too young and foolish to know it.

"Seeing ghosts?"

He turned his head, and there was Natasha, arranging herself on the seat beside him, her gold earrings swaying and her fringed shawl dragging the floor.

"You shouldn't have climbed all those bleacher steps."

"I knew you needed me."

He reached for her hand, then lifted it to his lips for a kiss.

"If you're planning to tell my fortune, Natasha, you can forget it. I've already thrown my future away."

"Your future is what you make it, Mick."

"I've been a fool."

"Everybody is at one time or another."

"I threw away the best thing that ever happened to me."

"Remember what Arthur used to say?" Her face softened and her eyes got misty.

Suddenly Mick saw all the times the three of them had spent together in a new light—the picnics after dark when the last performance was over; the quiet times with Arthur carving wooden animals and Natasha sitting nearby, mending her shawl; the lively times with Natasha spinning around a bonfire, doing a wild Gypsy dance and Arthur stamping his feet and clapping.

"You loved him, didn't you?"

"Yes. I loved him. He was my lover, my friend, and my companion." Natasha squeezed Mick's hand. "And you were the little boy we could never have."

Mick knew why. Arthur had a wife in Kentucky he'd never divorced.

"'Anything worth having is worth earning,'" he said, quoting Arthur. "He didn't take his own advice, did he?"

"No." Sasha leaned close, her black eyes boring into his. "She will take you back, you know. She loves you."

"How did you know about Tess?"

Natasha laughed. "I'm a fortune-teller, Mick. A *real* one."

He stood up, taking her hand. "Come with me, Natasha. You made me part of your family once; let me make you part of mine."

"Someday, maybe." When she tossed her shawl over her shoulders and shook her head, setting her gold earrings swinging, she looked twenty years younger. "But not yet. I have places to go and fortunes to tell."

Two weeks later Mick entered a small smoke-filled nightclub in Chicago.

Tess was on the stage, her head thrown back, her eyes closed, the mike held close to her lips as she sang "Stormy Weather." The blues lament sent shivers down Mick's spine. He stood in the doorway, spellbound.

Tess moved slowly across the stage, and the spotlight turned her to gold—her hair, her dress, her shoes. She was one bright, shimmering spot of gold, the gold at the end of his rainbow.

Tears of rejoicing wet his eyes, and he let them come, unashamed.

The song ended, and she took a deep bow to the applause. Mick started making his way to the front. When Tess looked up, she saw him. Her eyes went dark, and her hand whitened on the microphone.

Ever the consummate performer, she turned smoothly toward the piano, consulting her accompanist. The pianist played the opening bars.

Mick recognized the song, Gershwin, "Love Walked In." Tess was singing for him, to him. With her hips pressed against the piano, she sang, never moving, never taking her eyes off his.

The pianist took her smoothly from one Gershwin song straight to another, "Embraceable You." Mick's heart soared. Tess had always sent him messages in song. She was saying plainly, for all of Chicago to hear, "This is the man I love."

She ended her set to thunderous applause. Mick stood with the rest of the crowd, clapping the loudest of all.

She stood on the stage, taking her bows and watching Mick. When he had walked in, she had almost forgotten the words to her song. That had never happened to her before. Never.

Damn that unpredictable Irish wildcat. What was he doing in Chicago?

She made one last bow, then turned to leave the stage. She heard a small commotion, and turned in time to see Mick leap onto the stage. Her hand flew to her throat.

"What do you think you're doing?"

Instead of answering, he pulled her into his arms and kissed her, so thoroughly, so passionately, that by the time the kiss was over, he was practically holding her up.

The audience applauded.

"Damn you, Mick Flannigan." She pulled out of his embrace. "Who do you think you are to come waltzing back into my life again?"

"I'm the man who is going to marry you." His big Irish laughter boomed around the nightclub. "I'm planning to be your fourth and last husband."

She grabbed his hand and stormed off the stage pulling him with her. They sped down a narrow hallway and into a small dressing room. It had Tess's unmistakable stamp, silk and feathers strewn everywhere, jasmine perfume clinging to the air.

When they were inside, she slammed the door so hard the walls shook. Then she faced him, hands on her hips.

"I told you good-bye in Biloxi!" she shouted.

"No. *I* told you good-bye. I've changed my mind." He stalked her. She moved behind a chair.

"Don't you come a step closer."

"Why? Afraid you'll let me see how much you love me?"

"I don't love you anymore."

"That's not what you told me a while ago."

"That was a song. I was entertaining my audience."

"Believe me, Tess, I was entertained."

He shoved the chair aside and pulled her back into his arms.

"I've been a fool, Tess, my girl. You're all I want, all I've ever wanted. You're the gold at the end of my rainbow . . . and I've come to claim you."

"For how long this time, Mick? Two days? Two weeks? Maybe, if you don't get the itch to travel, two months?" She shoved at his chest. "No, thank you. I can live without that kind of heartbreak."

"Do you love me, Tess?" He caught her wrists

and wrapped her arms around his chest, hugging her tightly.

"This is not about love, Flannigan. This is about truth. And the truth is, I'm not going to be hurt by you anymore."

"Ahh, Tess. I will never hurt you again. Never."

His mouth closed over hers, and she was a helpless moth, flying into his flame. Her knees went weak, and her heart melted.

With his mouth and arms locked tightly on her, Mick backed across to the door and slid the bolt shut. It made a final clicking sound.

"No," she said, her mouth muffled against his. "I won't."

He lifted his head a fraction, smiling down at her. "You want me. Say you don't want me, and I'll leave."

"I don't want you. Leave." Even as she said those things, her hands were busy unbuttoning his shirt. Mick Flannigan was back and she had to have him, just one more time. "Go," she whispered, her hands on his belt buckle now. "Go chase another rainbow."

He stood still for a moment, watching her face as she undressed him, his eyes so bright they almost blinded her. Suddenly he exploded.

"Oh God, Tess! All those wasted years."

He hauled her into him and marched relentlessly toward a chaise longue littered with silk. They left a trail behind them, her gold-sequined shoes on his blue jeans, one of his boots under the hem of her dress, another boot tangled with her silk panties.

The fragile French antique protested as Flannigan braced one knee on the velvet cushions and lowered Tess to the pile of silk gowns. Red and blue and gold and purple bloomed behind her. She looked like an exotic flower with multicolored petals. He headed straight to the nectar.

With his eyes blazing down into hers, he slid home.

"Flannigan . . . Flannigan . . . Don't think this changes a thing," she said, her words spaced and breathless.

"It changes everything. This time you're mine. Forever."

"No."

"Yes. Forever."

The French antique rocked and groaned, and colored gowns went flying in all directions. They became frantic with passion and slick with sweat. Gaelic love words and the music of his name intermingled. Bodies and hearts intertwined.

They took the journey the long way around, and when they reached their destination, Flannigan sprawled back on the velvet cushions, taking her with him.

"You're mine, Tess. Mine. All mine," he said over and over, smoothing her damp hair back from her forehead.

"You gave up that claim long ago."

"I just restaked it."

"I'm afraid you missed."

"Shall I try again?"

With his dark curls plastered across his forehead and his wicked smile, he looked like a combination of a little boy with a new puppy and the devil himself. Tess had a hard time resisting him, but resist him she would.

She slipped out of his arms, and immediately felt the loss. She wasn't going to let it show, though. She didn't dare let him see how much she missed him already. Tossing her hair back, she faced him, naked and determined.

"I never give my former husbands a second time around." She bent gracefully and picked up one of her silk robes. It was red, the color of her flaming hair. She slid into the robe, then sat down at her dressing table and began to brush her hair.

She could see Flannigan watching her in the mirror. Damn his hide, he looked as satisfied as a big jungle cat.

"I can't say that I didn't enjoy our little reunion, Flannigan." She dragged the brush through her hair, heedless of tangles.

"I could see that, Tess, my girl." He chuckled.

"You were always good for a casual toss in the hay." He chuckled again. She wanted to throw the brush at him. Instead she kept brushing her hair.

"The next time you're passing through, Flannigan, give me a call. I might be in the market for a short-term lover."

"You'll have no more lovers, Tess, my girl. Only me."

She spun around, shaking the brush at him.

"How dare you come marching in here giving me orders! You have no right."

"I have every right. I love you."

"You told me that ten years ago. I'm too smart to believe it anymore."

He got up from the chaise longue and moved toward her, as relentless as Hannibal crossing the Alps. When he reached her, he caught her shoulders and bent her backward, forcing her to look up into his fierce face.

"I'll make you believe, Tess."

She wet her lips with her tongue. "No," she whispered.

"Don't be afraid, my love." Tenderly he traced her face with one finger. "I won't hurt you this time. As the saints are my witnesses, I will never leave you again."

She closed her eyes, needing to believe, wanting to believe. His fingers played softly over her face, and he began to croon to her—"The Irish Lullaby."

"Stop," she whispered. "Oh, please . . . stop."

"You love me, Tess. I can see it in your face."

"No."

"You do." His thumbs caressed the outline of her lips, then dipped inside and traced the moist inner lining.

Tess felt her will growing weaker. He was too close. His body heat was seducing her; his touch was distracting her. Oh God, she wanted him so. She wanted to believe every lying word he spoke.

But she could not. *Must* not. Bucking up her courage, she bit down on his finger.

He winced and withdrew his finger. Then he began to chuckle. "Do you think to be rid of me by inflicting pain?"

"I hope it hurt like hell." She spun back around and faced the mirror. He was reflected there, as bold as the devil and twice as dangerous.

"It did." He moved closer, putting his hands on her shoulders and leaning over so his face was next to hers, grinning back at her from the mirror. "You can leave teeth marks all over me, and I won't go away." His chuckle was wicked. "As a matter of fact, I'm thinking of a few good places I'd like you to sink your teeth."

She could too. And that was going to be a major problem. Especially if he decided to stick around. Oh Lord, how could she endure him this time, aching for him and knowing he'd leave again.

"You haven't even asked about Casey," she said suddenly.

Flannigan stepped back, pulled a cigar from his pocket, struck a match on his boot, and leaned against the edge of her dressing table, watching her through a haze of smoke.

"How is he?" he finally asked.

"Happy. Always cheerful, always optimistic."

"Is he good to you?"

"We're good to each other . . . and *for* each other. In many ways he's like the father I didn't have growing up. We've adopted each other." She sought his eyes through the smoke. "He always comes to my first show and sits in his special reserved seat; then he takes a cab home—back to my apartment."

She studied his face while she talked. He was intense, almost brooding, his eyes searching hers. She had to turn away from the contact. Looking back into the mirror, she began to apply a dusting of powder.

"Aunt Bertha has made her permanent home in Tupelo now, and who can blame her with Margaret Leigh and Andrew going to have their first baby soon and make her a grandmother?" She tossed the fluffy powder puff onto the dressing table. "As for me, I have Casey and O'Toole. We're a family—just the three of us."

"Are you telling me there's no room for one more?"

"Someday perhaps there will be room for one more. I don't like to be too long without a man." She stood up, watching to see how he had taken her last dig. She could see his black temper roiling just beneath the surface. Putting her hand on her hips, she turned and smiled at him. "But it won't be you, Flannigan."

His arm shot out and circled her waist. He dragged her roughly to him and positioned her between his widespread legs. It was like being sucked into the middle of a blazing furnace. She tipped her head back and glared defiantly into his eyes.

"These intimidation tactics aren't going to work, Flannigan."

"Every time you say my name that way, I know you want to make love, Tess."

He was right, but she'd be damned if she'd let him know it.

"Your ego is as big as your . . ."

"As big as my what, Tess. Go ahead. Say it." He was laughing.

"As big as your puffed-up head. Now, leave, Flannigan, before I get really mad."

His eyes darkened, and he bent her backward. With his lips on her throat he murmured, "I don't take orders, Tess." He kissed her throat until she shivered. Then, ever so gently, he brought her back upright and cradled her head against his shoulder. His hands sifted through her bright hair, and he watched it catch the light as it drifted through his fingers.

"One of the things I missed most about you through the years was your hair. The way it looks, the way it smells."

Leaning down, he pressed his face into her hair and inhaled. "I don't intend to be far away from the fragrance of your hair, Tess."

He leaned back from her, cupping her face so he could gaze directly into her eyes.

"I'm through chasing rainbows, Tess. Believe me."

"How can I?"

"What does your heart tell you to do?"

"I try not to listen to my heart anymore. It has

gotten me into trouble three times already. I can't afford a fourth mistake."

"It won't be a mistake. I promise you."

"You made promises ten years ago."

"I'm older now. I *know* what I want."

She was tempted. Flannigan had never looked or sounded more sincere. She was almost persuaded to believe him. She was almost convinced that they could put the past behind them and start all over again. Passion and fear rose in her, equally strong, and struggled a mighty battle. Fear won.

She stepped out of his arms. Holding on to the vanity chair for support, she faced him.

"Leave, Flannigan. And don't ever come back."

"I'll leave, Tess. But I'll be back. I promise you."

His exit was as bold as his entrance. Spangles and feather boas swayed with the breeze he created as he swept through the room. Even after the door had closed behind him, she could still hear the loud cannon-shot echoes of his boots as he marched down the hall.

"Damn him." She picked up her powder puff and threw it at the mirror. "Damn him, damn him, damn him." With one hand she raked all her cosmetics onto the floor. They landed in a crashing heap.

She sank to her knees among the gloss pots and lipsticks and eyeliners. She knew just how Atlanta had felt after Sherman marched through.

Her eyes strayed to the velvet chaise longue, and she burned to think how easily she'd given in to Flannigan. She shook a fist at the pile of silk gowns they'd knocked onto the floor.

"It won't happen again," she vowed. "I swear it. It will never happen again."

Eleven

Flannigan made himself comfortable on the sofa of Tess's apartment. Across from him, Casey sat in his easy chair, scratching O'Toole's back. Both the cat and the old man looked perfectly content.

"I figured you'd be coming back," Casey said.

"I didn't. I never planned to come back into Tess's life again."

"That day in the park, when I first overheard you talking, I said to myself, 'Now there's a fine pair of lovers who could use a good stabilizing influence.'"

"And so you decided to be that influence."

"Yes. I think it's worked out rather well. Don't you?"

"For you, it has. I have yet to convince Tess that I need to be a part of this family."

"You won't be long convincing her, or I miss my guess." Casey cocked his head, listening. "I hear her coming now." He rose from his chair, dumping O'Toole onto the floor. "'Tis best for an old man like me to be sound asleep when the fireworks start. And Flannigan . . . I want lots of grandchildren."

He winked, then walked down the hall toward his bedroom, O'Toole trailing along behind him.

Flannigan snapped off the lamp, then stretched his long legs out in front of him and lounged back against the cushions, watching the front door. Tess didn't see him when she first came through. He liked watching her unobserved. Her color was high, and she had the tousled, dewy look of a woman who has just made love. He wanted her all over again.

She tossed a sequined wrap toward the coatrack and missed. It fell into a gold heap on the hardwood floor. She leaned over and removed one sequined shoe, then made her way across the darkened room, walking lopsided in one high heel. When she reached the piano, she leaned over and ran one finger lightly down the keyboard. Her shoe dropped from her hand, and she sat down on the piano bench.

Humming softly, she began to chord. The chords became a melody, and soon Tess was leaning over the piano, crooning "It Had to Be You."

Flannigan sat in the dark, mesmerized. Her voice was satin and velvet and roses and moonlight. And he knew beyond a shadow of a doubt that she was singing for him, even without knowing he was there.

He closed his eyes, letting the honeyed sounds of her voice sink into his scarred soul. "I'm home," he said to himself. "I've finally come home."

The last note of the song died away, and they both sat in the dark, Tess leaning over the keyboard and Flannigan watching her. Finally she sighed and turned her head.

Flannigan clapped softly. "Bravo, Tess. You're magnificent."

"Flannigan?" She rose from the piano bench,

and made her way to him. "Is that you, Flannigan?"

"I told you I would never leave you, Tess." He rose from the sofa and faced her. "I don't intend to."

She stopped and planted her hands on her hips. "Where's Casey?"

"Gone to bed. I think I hear him snoring already."

"He should have thrown you out. You abandoned both of us in Biloxi."

"I will not abandon you again . . . either of you."

He crossed the space that separated them, and pulled her gently into his arms.

"I want to spend the rest of my life with you. I want us to have lots of children and cats and dogs. I want us to sit beside our own fireplace and hold hands and laugh together. I want us to grow old together." He pressed his face into her hair. "I want to die with you and be buried with you. I want to journey into the afterworld still joined to you, still loving you." His lips grazed her forehead, the top of her head. "Tess, my girl. I love you so."

Tears sprang to her eyes, but she batted them away. Standing in Mick's arms, she allowed herself to dream for a moment, and then she pushed him away.

"I don't suppose you have a place to sleep?"

"No," he said.

"How like you, Flannigan, to assume that all you had to do was show your face and I'd invite you to my bed." She switched on the lamp and began to toss sofa cushions onto the floor. "This makes a bed. You can sleep here."

He gave her a triumphant smile as he made the sofa into a bed.

"Only for tonight. Tomorrow, you leave." He

began to whistle. "I mean it, Flannigan. Tomorrow you're out of my life . . . for good."

With that final word she left him in her den, whistling and getting his bed ready for the night. She went into her bedroom and slammed the door.

What right had he to disrupt her life again? What made him think she would come running back to him after all these years? Her gold-sequined gown fell into a heap on the rug, and she kicked it aside. Naked and enraged, she marched to the shower. She locked the bathroom door behind her. Nowhere was safe from Flannigan. It would be just like him to pick the lock and climb into her shower. The last time he'd been wearing his boots.

She leaned against the wall, weak, as she remembered the way he had come to her in Biloxi. Water washed over her unheeded.

"Damn you, Flannigan. Why did you have to come back?"

She leaned her head against the tiles. They were cold, just like her life. Sterile, just like her life. She squeezed her eyes shut, holding back tears. She wouldn't cry now. Not while he was here. She'd cry tomorrow, after he had gone.

She finished her shower quickly and climbed into her lonely bed. She heard stirrings through the door. Flannigan would be sprawled on the sofa, the sheet twisted around his torso, exposing his muscular legs. He never liked to keep his legs under the covers, even in wintertime. She guessed that was because he was always poised to run.

He had said he was through running. Was he telling the truth? Was it possible that, after all these years, Flannigan was ready to settle down?

"It's not my problem," she muttered, twisting herself in her sheets.

He had said he'd found what he wanted. He

wanted a family and children and pets and a home with a fireplace.

Suddenly she sat up in bed and switched on her lamp. Propped against her headboard, she studied her bedroom. It was filled with the trappings of her career—the closet full of glittery costumes, the musical scores spread upon her dressing table, the yellow roses sent by fans, their leaves beginning to turn brown and curl at the edges.

She was successful and admired and fawned over. And she was as lonely as hell.

She arose from her bed and began to pace the floor. She loved singing, loved her career; and Casey helped fill the void. But the happiest days of her life had been ten years ago when she and Mick were living in a walk-up apartment, laughing over which one of them would have enough money to pay the next light bill.

Her footsteps faltered, and then she was running, running toward the bedroom door. She shoved it open and waited for her eyes to adjust to the darkness. Mick was spread across the sofa bed, just the way she knew he would be.

Smiling, she started his way. When she was close enough, she leaned down and ran her hand under the sheet.

"Hmm. No clothes. How convenient."

"Tess?" He sat up, running his hands through his tousled hair and yawning. "Tess? Is that you?"

"Who were you expecting? The queen of England?"

She burrowed under the covers and planted nibbling kisses down his right leg. He pulled the sheet over them and wrapped her in his arms.

"Sure and it's good to have you back in my bed, Tess, my girl." Chuckling, he nuzzled her neck.

"Don't get your hopes up. This is just a trial run."

"Then let's make it a good one."

He lay back and settled her over his hips. They came together with the explosive fury of a summer storm. And when the storm was spent, they lay back against his pillows, clinging to each other as if they had just discovered the only life vest on a sinking ship.

"Does this mean you'll marry me, Tess, my girl?"

"No."

"No?" He leaned away, trying to see her face in the dark. "You came to my bed and loved me like that, and you're telling me no?"

"I'm saying no to marriage. I'm not saying no to an extended affair."

"Another trial run?"

"You might call it that."

"What if I said no. What if I said the only way I'll have you is as my wife?"

"Take it or leave it, Flannigan."

"And where might you be wanting this affair to take place?"

"Where might you be wanting to have this little cottage with all the dogs and cats and children?"

"How does Texas sound to you?"

"With bluebonnets?"

"And a small flying school."

Tess sat up and reached for her gown. "I've always wanted to give Texas a whirl."

She arose from the bed, and he didn't try to stop her. There would be a way to get her to marry him. Right now he wouldn't press. He'd take this one step at a time.

Propping his hands behind his head, he smiled up at her.

"Suppose we do find a little cottage in a field,

and I start a flying school. What will you be doing, Tess . . . besides decorating and warming my bed?"

"I can sing anywhere." Waving her hands in the air, she watched him closely. "Who knows? I might chuck everything and become an unknown, a has-been giving lessons in the parlor of a small Texas cottage."

"I might take a lesson or two myself, Tess, my girl."

She felt as if she'd just been awarded a Grammy.

"Well . . ." She lingered beside his sofa bed awhile longer, and then she started toward her own bed. " 'Night, Flannigan."

"Good night, Tess."

Tess stood at the window, watching and waiting. A painted sunset made a backdrop for the man coming up the path. His shoulders were broad, his step was jaunty, and he was whistling. Flannigan. He whistled a lot of late. In fact, he'd been whistling for two weeks now, ever since they'd left Chicago and moved to Texas, with Casey and O'Toole in tow.

Tess's heart climbed into her throat as Flannigan approached the door, and she had to remind herself that this was only a trial run. She hadn't made any commitment, and didn't intend to. No marriage vows, no heartbreak. That's the way she looked at it. Oddly enough, Flannigan never pressed the issue.

The door opened, and he stepped through, bringing the heat of the summer evening with him. She ran to him, arms outstretched. He scooped her up and waltzed her around the room.

"Did you have a good day, Tess, my girl?"

"Yes. I got my first students, cousins. Elena Rae and Sukie Mae Glenn."

"And can they sing?" He still waltzed her around the room. Her head was spinning, but he didn't appear the least bit dizzy.

"Like Hereford cattle. But wait until I've finished with them." He nuzzled her neck, still waltzing round and round. "Mick, put me down. My head is spinning."

"Anything for my girl."

He sank into their rocking chair and held her on his lap. She ran her hands through his hair and smiled into his eyes.

"And how was your day, Mick Flannigan?"

"I'm on my way to becoming the most famous flying teacher in all of Texas."

"Why?"

"Because the mayor of this fair town is my first student. That's why."

"That calls for a celebration." Tess slid off his lap and caught the side of the rocking chair.

"Tess?" Mick grabbed her arm. "Are you all right?"

"Too much dancing round and round." She took two deep breaths, then smiled at him. "I guess I'm getting old."

"Then marry me before you get any older."

It was the first time he had mentioned marriage since they'd come to Texas.

"You know my position on that, Mick."

"And you know mine."

Their eyes locked, and both of them felt a battle coming on. It would be their first in a long, long time.

"You'll leave again," she said, her chin outthrust. "You always do."

She saw his quick anger boil to the surface. His

eyes sparkled, and his jaw clenched. Then, just as suddenly as it had come, the anger died away.

He reached out and tenderly traced the side of her jaw.

"Don't be thinking I'll ever leave you, Tess, my girl." His fingers moved across her lips. "Or disapprove of you." He bent his head close. "Or try to change you." His lips were so close and she could feel his warm breath across her cheek. "I love you . . . just the way you are. Always have and always will. It took me a long time to figure it out."

She closed her eyes and let herself go limp. Suddenly he scooped her in his arms and strode down the hallway.

"Casey and O'Toole will be back from their walk soon," she said.

Flannigan kicked the bedroom door shut behind them. "Casey knows to respect a closed door."

They left a trail of clothes all the way to the bed.

The days grew shorter, and fall began to nip the air. In the cottage beside Ray Hubbard Lake outside Dallas, Casey and O'Toole sat watching their favorite game show, while Tess strained her eyes to see down the dark path.

Flannigan was late. He'd never been this late. She stilled the panic that began to rise in her chest. This very moment he could be winging his way south, leaving her and Casey and O'Toole to pick up their lives and go on without him.

"No." She clutched her middle, moaning.

"Did you say something?" Casey looked up from his game show.

"I was just humming." Tess walked away from the window, humming a jazzy tune under her breath. Oh dear God, not now. Flannigan couldn't leave now.

The front door banged open, and in walked Flannigan, his arms loaded and face split with a huge grin.

"Top of the evening." He grinned at her over his armload. "Come and give me a kiss, Tess, my girl. I can't get to you with all this stuff."

Relief made her legs weak as she leaned over the hammer and wood and dowels and screws and gave him a warm welcome-home kiss.

"What is all this?" she asked as she stepped back.

"My new hobby." He dumped his supplies in the middle of the floor. "Wood carving." He began to sort through the mess, whistling.

"Wood carving? It looks as if you're planning to build the Taj Mahal."

"No. I'm building a cradle—for Jenny." Her face turned pale, and she clutched the back of the rocking chair, but Flannigan didn't seem to notice. He was puttering around his pile of tools, sorting and whistling.

He looked up, smiling. "Do you think she'd like roses carved along the headboard?"

"Who?" Tess whispered.

"Jenny." He spoke matter-of-factly, as if only yesterday they had discussed what they would name their firstborn daughter.

"Aren't you presuming a lot?"

"No. I'm planning on being a father." Flannigan turned back to the pile of lumber that would be a cradle and began to whistle again.

Tess's hands balled into fists, and she stalked toward him. "And who might you be planning to be the mother Flannigan?"

He stood up and bracketed her shoulders. "You, my love."

"I never said I'd marry you, let alone bear your children."

She stood glaring at him, nose to nose. He didn't back down an inch.

Casey, sensing a storm, picked up O'Toole and left quietly, by the back door.

"Ahh, Tess." Flannigan leaned closer and brushed his lips across hers.

"Don't." She jerked her head back. "Don't get me sidetracked."

He cupped her face. "How long were you going to wait to tell me, Tess, my girl?"

"Tell you what?"

"Did you think you could keep the secret forever?"

"What secret?"

"Ahh, my stubborn Tess." Flannigan moved closer, caressing her cheeks as he talked. "I've seen the changes in your body, my love." He flattened one hand across her abdomen. "I know you carry my child here, in your womb."

With his hand over her womb, pressing gently against the precious burden she carried there, Tess melted. She'd known for weeks that she was pregnant. Each day she had waited for Flannigan to grow restless and walk out the door. And each day when he came back, she breathed a prayer of thanksgiving.

And now he was building a cradle—for Jenny. She wanted to give in. She wanted to grab her dream with both hands and hold on tight. For she knew, at long, long last, that what she wanted most in the world was Flannigan and all the things he had to offer—the passion, the humor, the gentleness, the brooding, even the longing for adventure she sometimes saw lurking in his eyes.

Ten years ago they had set out on their journey together, then had got separated and visited different places; and now they were back on the same train, going to the same destination. She didn't ever want to leave the train again, but she had to make certain that Flannigan was on board for the right reasons—and for the duration.

"We live in a modern age, Flannigan. A man is no longer obligated to marry the mother of his child."

"Obligated?" His hands gripped her shoulders, and he crushed her so close, her head was forced back. "Did you say *obligated*?" Thunder and lightning flashed just behind his eyes.

"That's what I said. A woman has choices."

"If you think I'd let you go, you'd best reconsider."

"Because of Jenny?"

"Because of *you*." He bent so close, his lips were almost touching hers. "I've waited, Tess . . . waited for you to come to your senses . . ."

"Come to my senses!"

". . . and marry me." He moved a fraction closer so that his lips grazed hers. "I've waited for you to know that I'll never leave you, that I'll always love you, no matter what you do." Suddenly he scooped her up into his arms. "I'm waiting no more, Tess."

"What are you going to do?" He said nothing, but marched resolutely from the room. "Flannigan, put me down."

He ignored her. His boots thundered against the hardwood floor as he made his way to their bedroom.

She looked at his face and then at the bed.

"We can't always settle our differences here, Flannigan."

He lowered her to the bed, then straightened up

and ripped aside his shirt. Buttons went flying all over the room.

"Who says I'm settling differences?" He sat on the edge of the bed, and his boots clattered to the floor. Next he peeled out of his tight jeans. Naked, Flannigan was a magnificent sight.

"If you think you can win me with your body, Flannigan, you're wrong." Even as Tess spoke, she was lifting her arms toward him.

"Who says I'm winning you?" His eyes blazed as he ran his hands up her skirt and tore aside her tiny silk bikinis. With his hands under her hips, he lifted her to meet his thrust. When he was home, settled deep inside her, he propped himself on his elbows and gazed down into her eyes.

"I'm taking you captive, my love."

"Flannigan." He began to move, and the earth spun away.

"I'm planning to stay here, in this bedroom with you under me, until you say 'yes.'"

"Flannigan . . . Flannigan."

"Is that a yes?"

"Will you go away if I say yes this soon?"

"No. I'll never go away." His movements became fierce and possessive. "Never."

"Then, yes, Flannigan." She wrapped her arms around him and held him close. "Yes."

He gave her the smile that had been designed by angels.

"I think I'll keep you captive anyhow, Tess, my girl."

Epilogue

Tess and Mick Flannigan established a tradition that the birth of each child would be celebrated with a huge welcome-to-the-world party.

Baby Casey Flannigan lay in his crib, hand-carved by his father, and observed the crowd who had come to celebrate his birth. He knew them all by name, for he was the smartest baby boy in all of Texas. That's what his daddy had told him, and he believed it. He was also the handsomest. His mother had told him that, and he believed her too.

There was Johnny Kalinopolis, the tall, gray-haired man standing beside the mantel. He was talking to Lovey and Jim Hawkins and a pretty little dark-haired girl named Babs. Casey thought he might grow up and marry Babs. He fancied himself as a man of the world who might love an older woman someday.

Baby Casey had lots of cousins—Andy and Maggie, the twins, then Joey and baby Elaine. Baby Elaine blew spit bubbles all the time. Casey was hoping she'd teach him how.

All his cousins belonged to Aunt Margaret Leigh

and Uncle Andrew McGill. Aunt Margaret Leigh was his mother's sister, and she was very nice, but he liked his uncle Andrew best. He smelled like leather and pine woods, and he'd promised Casey a bird-dog puppy when he was six. He hoped it didn't take too long to get six.

A very old woman called Aunt Bertha sat in the rocking chair beside his crib, and she had said she was his grandmother. He doubted that, but if it made her happy, he'd go along. His *real* grandparents were on the love seat beside the bay windows, holding hands—Casey and Natasha. Natasha jingled when she walked, and Casey talked funny, like music. They lived together in a little cottage behind Baby Casey's big white house. His daddy had told him Casey and Natasha were very special people who had met and fallen in love when Baby Casey's oldest sister was born.

Baby Casey had three sisters, but his oldest sister was his favorite. Micki and Susan were nice if you liked rowdy, dark-headed sisters, but Jenny was still the best. She had blue eyes that looked like the sky and pretty red hair that glowed in the sunlight. And she was always singing.

Baby Casey loved for Jenny to lean over his crib and sing a lullaby. Her voice was almost as pretty as his mother's.

Baby Casey twisted around so he could see his mother, Tess. She was standing in the open doorway, shading her face against the sunlight and looking up into the sky. He guessed when he went somewhere with his bird-dog puppy and his mother, everybody would sit up and take notice, for it was certain she'd be the most beautiful mother there.

Suddenly Baby Casey heard a roar in the sky, and his mother left the doorway. Baby Casey grunted with the effort of rolling his head sideways so he could see her out the window. She was running across a field of bluebonnets with her arms outstretched.

Baby Casey's big, handsome daddy stepped down from the cockpit, threw off his helmet, and began to run. Tess and Flannigan met in the middle of the field of flowers, and Flannigan lifted her high in the air. They stayed that way for a long time, and it looked as if they were dancing.

Then Flannigan lowered Tess to the ground and bent over her. They were kissing. Baby Casey knew because they did it all the time.

It looked like an awful lot of fun. He couldn't wait until he got big enough to try it.

•

THE EDITOR'S CORNER

It's going to be a merry month, indeed, for all of us LOVESWEPT devotees with romances that are charming, delightful, moving, and hot!

First, one of Deborah Smith's most romantic, dreamy love stories ever, CAMELOT, LOVESWEPT #468. Deb sweeps you away to sultry Florida, a setting guaranteed to inspire as much fantasizing in you as it does in heroine Agnes Hamilton. The story opens on a stormy night when Agnes has been thinking and dreaming about the love story recorded in the diary of a knight of Britain's Middle Ages. He seems almost real to her. When the horses on her breeding farm need her help to shelter from the wind and rain, Agnes forges out into the night—only to meet a man on horseback who seems for all the world like her knight of old. Who is the wickedly handsome John Bartholomew and dare she trust their instant attraction to each other? This is a LOVESWEPT to read slowly so you can enjoy each delicious phrase of a beautiful, sensual, exciting story.

Welcome a marvelous new talent to our fold, Virginia Leigh, whose SECRET KEEPER, LOVESWEPT #469, is her first published novel. Heroine Mallory Bennett is beautiful, sexy—and looking her worst in mud-spattered jeans (sounds like real life, huh?), when hero Jake Gallegher spots her in the lobby of his restaurant. From the first he knows she's Trouble . . . and he senses a deep mystery about her. Intrigued, he sets out to probe her secrets and find the way to her heart. Don't miss this moving and thrilling love story by one of our New Faces of '91!

Joan Elliott Pickart is back with a funny, tender, sizzler, MEMORIES, LOVESWEPT #470. This is an irresistible story of a second chance at love for Minty Westerly and Chism Talbert. Minty grew up happy and privileged;

Chism grew up troubled and the caretaker's son. But status and money couldn't come between them for they had all the optimism of the young in love. Then Chism broke Minty's heart, disappearing on the same night they were to elope. Now, back in town, no longer an angry young man, but still full of passion, Chism encounters Minty, a woman made cautious by his betrayal. Their reunion is explosive—full of pain and undimmed passion . . . and real love. You'll revel in the steps this marvelous couple takes along the path to true love!

That marvelous romantic Linda Cajio gives you her best in EARTH ANGEL, LOVESWEPT #471, next month. Heroine Catherine Wagner is a lady with a lot on her mind—rescuing her family business from a ruthless and greedy relative while pursuing the cause of her life. When she meets charismatic banker Miles Kitteridge she thinks he must be too good to be true. His touch, his fleeting kisses leave her weak-kneed. But is he on to her game? And, if so, can she trust him? Miles knows he wants the passionate rebel in his arms forever . . . but capturing her may be the toughest job of his life! A real winner from Linda!

Welcome another one of our fabulous New Faces of '91, Theresa Gladden, with her utterly charming debut novel, ROMANCING SUSAN, LOVESWEPT #472. First, devastatingly handsome Matt Martinelli steals Susan Wright's parking space—then he seems determined to steal her heart! And Susan fears she's just going to be a pushover for his knock-'em-dead grin and gypsy eyes. She resists his lures . . . but when he gains an ally in her matchmaking great aunt, Susan's in trouble—delightfully so. A love story of soft Southern nights and sweet romancing that you'll long remember!

Patt Bucheister strikes again with one of her best ever sensual charmers, HOT PURSUIT, LOVESWEPT #473. Rugged he-man Denver Sierra is every woman's dream and a man who will not take no for an answer. Lucky Courtney Caine! But it takes her a while to realize just how lucky she is. Courtney has hidden in the peaceful shadows cast by her performing family. Denver is determined to draw her out into the bright sunshine of life . . . and to melt her icy fears with the warmth of his affection and the fire of his desire. Bravo, Patt!

We trust that as always you'll find just the romances you want in all six of our LOVESWEPTs next month. Don't forget our new imprint, FANFARE, if you want more of the very best in women's popular fiction. On sale next month from FANFARE are three marvelous novels that we guarantee will keep you riveted. MORTAL SINS is a mesmerizing contemporary novel of family secrets, love, and unforgettable intrigue from a dynamic writing duo, Dianne Edouard and Sandra Ware. THE SCHEMERS by Lois Wolfe is a rich, thrilling historical novel set during the Civil War with the most unlikely—and marvelous—heroine and hero. She's a British aristocrat, he's a half-Apache army scout. Be sure also to put Joan Dial's sweeping historical FROM A FAR COUNTRY on your list of must-buy fiction. This enthralling novel will take you on a romantic journey between continents . . . and the hearts and souls of its unforgettable characters.

Ah, so much for you to look forward to in the merry month ahead.

Warm good wishes,

Carolyn Nichols

Carolyn Nichols
Editor
LOVESWEPT
Bantam Books
666 Fifth Avenue
New York, NY 10102-0023

60 Minutes to a Better, More Beautiful You!

Now it's easier than ever to awaken your sensuality, stay slim forever—even make yourself irresistible. With Bantam's bestselling subliminal audio tapes, you're only 60 minutes away from a better, more beautiful you!

__	45004-2	**Slim Forever**	$8.95
__	45035-2	**Stop Smoking Forever**	$8.95
__	45022-0	**Positively Change Your Life**	$8.95
__	45041-7	**Stress Free Forever**	$8.95
__	45106-5	**Get a Good Night's Sleep**	$7.95
__	45094-8	**Improve Your Concentration**	$7.95
__	45172-3	**Develop A Perfect Memory**	$8.95

Bantam Books, Dept. LT, 414 East Golf Road, Des Plaines, IL 60016

Please send me the items I have checked above. I am enclosing $_____ (please add $2.50 to cover postage and handling). Send check or money order, no cash or C.O.D.s please. (Tape offer good in USA only.)

Mr/Ms _____

Address _____

City/State _____ Zip _____

LT-2/91

Please allow four to six weeks for delivery.
Prices and availability subject to change without notice.

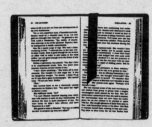